MW00323024

Say Hey Little Prince

Say Hey Little Prince

A Novel

Steven Dandaneau

Owl Canyon Press

First Edition, 2020

All Rights Reserved

Dandaneau, Steven

Say Hey Little Prince —1st ed.

Library of Congress Control Number: 2020945666

p. cm.

ISBN: 978-1-952085-02-4

Owl Canyon Press

Boulder, Colorado

Dedication

In memory of Antoine de Saint-Exupéry

Each individual is a miracle.–*Wind, Sand and Stars* (1939)
Your son is in a burning house. (…) It is the rescue of your child that
is you–*Flight to Arras* (1942)
Grief takes my breath away.–*Wartime Writings*, 1939-1944 (1982)

List of Main Characters

The Little Prince..............................….. a pitcher of baseballs
Jim Murry…….....…....................……...a baseball team manager
Mrs. Stefanski (Mrs. S.) ....…......... a team owner, widow

List of Secondary Characters

Seth Franken ....…..................…......a play-by-play broadcaster
Hector Gonzalez ....…..a baseball broadcast color analyst
Moisés Saramachi ....…..........a baseball team manager
Sage One ....…...................…...................... a sports writer
Sage Two ....…......a more human than not sports writer
Reginald Ross ....…....…..... a man
Reggie Ross ....…...… a young man
Lucy Higgins ....…....…... a fouled-ball girl
Sammy Robertson ....…...…... a catcher of baseballs
Jeff Millsaps ....…...… a pitching coach
Earl Stefanski ....…................…....… Mrs. S.'s brother
Dave Shoal ...…....................................…..... a general manager
Akihiko Sato.......................…....................…...... an established ace
Walker Evans Stefanski ....…...…...… Mrs. S.'s nephew
Sam Sweetwater ....…....…...… Mrs. S's doctor
Mary Sweetwater ....…....…....…... Sam's daughter
Maria Higgins ....….............…...… Lucy's mother
Dan Higgins ....…....…... Lucy's father
Harold Morris ....…....…....… .an Olympic medalist
Hud ....….... not like the others
Mr. S...................…...................................…....…...… a visionary

ONE

Rosy comes to mind.

Rozema. Don't forget Fidrych. The Bird's the word, Seth.

It's our story, Hector. A rookie starter. Perhaps a Phenom.

Oh, it's a wild story, Seth.

It brings back memories.

It's before our time, but he has me thinking about Schoolboy Rowe.

That *is* going back.

He's so green, Seth, he's Mean Joe Greene. He's stout. But never to no one's knowledge even started in the *minors*. It's like what they say, unprecedented.

He's maybe the next Newhouser.

He's unprecedented, Seth.

I'm sure we're going to be talking about this young pitcher for a while, but, first, what's running through a manager's mind about now.

I don't know. This is not a desperate team. They have a veteran at nearly every position, a dangerous offense. And, sure, their pen isn't as consistent as they want and their starting five's been up and down, but they're not a team afraid of anyone.

The sun may be in a few eyes, Hector, but it's a glorious afternoon for baseball.

***

Mrs. S. called him the Little Prince. Hal Newhouser had been her late-husband's favorite ballplayer. When Mr. S. was growing up, Newhouser was Prince Hal to Mr. S. and millions of adoring fans. Now Mrs. S. owned the team, although she herself didn't care about baseball. Her disinterest profound, Mrs. S. wasn't familiar with an alternative pitching great to whom she might as well have alluded, through whose example she might have expressed her affection. She didn't care for the Little Prince's given name either, which was Over-the-Rhine, a name more appropriate for a German Shepherd than a prince, she said. He wasn't little. He wasn't, like Newhouser, left-handed. He wasn't black or white or broadcast in living color. The Little Prince was Mrs. S.'s adopted boy wonder. In her way of seeing things, he was mysterious by design. Mrs. S. hoped beyond hope that the Little Prince would one day be her *enfant extraordinaire*.

***

Is it true what I heard

    Yes, we're starting him.

    When's he warming up.

    He doesn't warm up.

    Really. He doesn't warm up.

    When he comes out, he's ready to go.

    You say when he comes out, you want to start.

    Yes, Durwood, we'll send him out when it's time to start.

    If that's what you want, Jim.

    It's not about what I want, Durwood. It's just the way it is.

***

Mrs. Margaret L. Stefanski met the Little Prince when he was a middle-schooler. He overshared that he had been orphaned at age six and seven:

one parent died two weeks before and the other two weeks after his seventh birthday. Mrs. S. looked at him blankly, although not unsympathetically, as he explained that both deaths originated in the same catastrophe. Based on her expression and his already developed sense for these things, the precocious Little Prince spared Mrs. S. his theory that their separation deepened the impact the way an atomic explosion begins with blast, followed by heat, and then radiation. That the Little Prince wept at neither funeral was the result of shellshock, not indifference. Those rituals left him feeling a permanent stranger.

Even though the Little Prince rarely spoke of orphan status (he did not apply the term to himself, even when others did), it wasn't that he lacked a need and desire to share of himself, of his innermost thoughts and feelings. But what the Little Prince discovered pretty quickly was that no one he knew seemed to have much curiosity, or if they did, the ability, to hear his story and respond to it, not so much appropriately, as meaningfully, with care and genuine understanding. He greatly enjoyed others and found all things human fascinating. And he never gave up hope of landing connection. The last, after all, wasn't really an option.

Sometimes the Little Prince would make a cautious approach, to assess someone's openness to openness, but this usually resulted in palpable discomfort. Interlocutors might become distant and mute; just as often they would hold out shiny distractions. As he explored human life on earth, the Little Prince discovered that people spent a lot of time donning happy faces when not engaged in one or another artificial distraction. The Little Prince came increasingly to think of this indirection as indiscretion, as purposeful avoidance of truth, in crucial ways, as avoidance of life itself.

The Little Prince could not, and would never, escape childhood images and elementary understandings that were for him, like for all people, foundations of his adolescent psyche. For the Little Prince, it was not odd to empathize with people in Hiroshima and Nagasaki whose summertime shadows had been cast in city sidewalks. It was not strange to feel for the human in the pilots who flew those missions or in other serial killers. The Little Prince did not believe in what people called evil, if by that they referred to something extraterrestrial. In school, the Little Prince tested well for cognitive ability, but what set him apart, in his own mind especially, was his need to see things critically, to see the not-yet in others, to see the world as it was as well as potentially anew. As it turned out, he was an excellent athlete, but all that truly mattered to the Little Prince was what it meant to live as a human being.

***

Mrs. S. encountered her Little Prince during a diplomatic tour of the Syracuse Boys & Girls Club when around a corner stood a handsome and sturdy lad with Steinbeck in his hands. As she saw it, an initial conversation, focused and intense, led to something more in-depth on a second visit. Several trips and court orders later and Mrs. S.'s charge was on course to one expensive youth enrichment program, sports camp, and young writer's workshop after another. From her intermittent perspective, Mrs. S.'s adopted stripling ping ponged through adolescence with indeterminate greatness. The Little Prince's telos was always tantalizingly out of reach, the way light from Alpha Centauri, the nearest star to our solar system, takes over four years to reach Earth.

***

The Little Prince grew and his and Mrs. S.'s relationship evolved and deepened. In time, a teen moved to an apartment leased in Mrs. S.'s attorney's cousin's name, in the city in which Mrs. S. was known as an auto-mall baroness and the widow who inherited a middling yet much beloved major league professional baseball franchise. Despite questionable decisions on the automobile side, Mrs. S. received positive reviews when she left in place the team's old man of the sea, its manager, Jim Murry, for whom there was equally diffuse local affection.

***

Gentleman, I've got your line-up cards. There's a lot of extra stuff today but TV says we start when the centerfield clock shows 1:07. Moisés, you okay with that.

Sure, it's good. We're all good, Mister Durwood. Feeling great.

Okay then, we'll start when Jim's boy takes the mound. At 1:07.

Good luck, Mister Jim. Good to be in your house, my friend.

It sure is warm today my friends, but I expect we'll all survive.

Jimmy, you say your guy doesn't warm up. You mean, not at all.

***

Jim Murry and his yard—the mass entertainment baseball complex at which he had been a fixture for more than two decades—were past their respective primes and all three: expensive, expansive, and irregular. Given its year of construction, *Stade de Stefanski* featured oddly uneven lines and alleys, what the late Mr. S. said was the inevitable albeit not displeasing result of its having been sited amid so many downtown edifices. One of the city's most strident sports authoritarian personalities begged to differ. He claimed to know that the unnatural outcome was preordained by selection of an atheistic French architect raised, so the urban legend went, on fútbol and *théorie sociale postmoderne*. It was never clear which alien source he thought more damning.

Left and centerfield were St. Paul's and St. Peter's, respectively, but right field flirted with excommunication. In addition to its uniquely uncomfortable proximity to home plate, right field featured an indentation, what amounted to a Maginot Line for hitters. Were it in their power—pull-hitters of the gauchiste variety especially—they would swing in hope of driving pitches to either side of the indentation, a trajectory that could save ten-to-twenty feet of Ardennes Forest. Many pursued this strategy only to send balls straight into the deepest point of indentation, drawing not a few comparisons to golf. Some batters threw their bats into the pond and swore they would never bat again.

The two most learned sports writers in the city were also perhaps the two most learned sports writers in the country. They dubbed right-center field Belgium. They named the area between the indentation and the shortest ticket to ride in any major league park, the merely 289-foot right field line, Little Belgium. After every quip about Belgium or Little Belgium, they would wink as if to say, *entre nous*. Curiously, the indentation itself hadn't earned a consistently applied nickname. A mean-spirited few called it Jim Murry's gap tooth. Hit it in the gap, they shouted.

Knowing their editors, the two sports writers—Baseball Aficionado and Baseball Maven—never tossed these or similar bon mots, of which they produced a steady diet, into their copy. They refrained even in op/eds and thought pieces. Editors Bud Roper and Dick Howell, unwitting yet loving devotees of Newspeak, encouraged all nationally recognized sportswriters with whom they worked exactly never in this or that direction.

Dick and Bud insisted upon transparency. Write so we can see through your windows, they would say, which in practice meant short sentences. If they reviewed a sentence with stores of meaning laid-in over multiple clauses, they would type a simple directive—make it transparent; I don't follow—and hit return to sender.

This rive practice (perhaps it was better described as a *policy*, a damnable blanking policy), was considered by writerly sages everywhere—especially at well-oiled sage conclaves and conventions—as tantamount to industry-wide knuckling to mass subscriber intellectual atrophy. They had already dumbed down their prose to conform to standard eighth grade public reading proficiency. This policy, this stylistic oppression, this abdication of literary *duty*, they hummed in unison, drained joy from their chosen artform, their beloved vocation. How much joy, Dick and Bud queried. Much joy.

This was true even when their daily output could be expanded and bound into books. Sage One's and Sage Two's respective winter bestsellers continued to be gifted year-around on birthdays and other occasions when no one knew what to get dad. Yet, even these projects required extensive editing for accessibility, intelligibility, and market. Each year seemed more dispiriting than the previous. If only they could experience what was once taken for granted by a Roger Angell, a Stephen Jay Gould, or a George Will.

Ostensible competitors, baseball journalism's Queen of Sheba and Duke of Kakiak agreed that the holiday book market was anymore Chanukah in a handbasket. But they likewise agreed that wise men should soldier on, not resigned to the privileged grind of making, or finding, meaning in sport. Yet, who among them was a wise man.

***

During not a few English Oval-chewed postgame bull sessions hosted in his surprisingly opulent stadium office, Jim Murry might announce, as though he hadn't said it to the same group two weeks prior, that the main scoreboard in centerfield was so garish that it might as well say Trump on it (and he feared that someday it would). On occasions when he was in moods foreboding—offshore spill moods, Red Adair moods, moods which Jim might lighten with puffs of knowing wit and wisdom as airy as his thinning gray hair—when Jim was in moods of this tenor and ilk, he might pontificate in ways that presented his acumen in a more favorable light than it may have deserved. He might say, for example: as mangers past learned in due time but as I surmised *day one* (pausing, eyes ablaze above kiln-dried mustache), it helps immeasurably, my friends, to have a bona fide Olympic medalist in centerfield.

On a Saturday afternoon around the Fourth of July, Jim might have a team and tens-of-thousands of guests over for a contest of wits staged on diamond dust and grass. Certain writers bored senseless by stretches of baseball inaction might deign to entertain themselves by lavishing attention on Jim's exceptionally fleet centerfielder. He was a Bronze Man. His territory Grant Park. His mission to recapture past glory taste-testing gelato with an infinite supply of gelato-tasting spoons. He had a golden contract and was destined to hasten realization of world peace if only Ole Quicksilver could hit as well as he could lay conquest to vast reaches of Bermuda and rye. Entre nous.

***

It appeared that whoever mowed the outfield was afflicted by attention deficit and hyperactivity disorder. The organist partially compensated for the mowing, as data revealed from annual surveys of patron satisfaction. The water features—planned and subsequently managed by a third party, Fan Favorite, LLC—were so deep and mild that never a year passed without some number diving, falling, or otherwise being drawn into them. Lit and aerated, their various and sundry pools were populated by an incalculable universe of tiny multitudinous luminescent bubbles, so many spare stars from so many round holes, perhaps enough, rarified speculation held, to fill The Royal Albert Hall.

This is the sort of thing about which sports journalists might write. These are men and women who choose to apply their talents in the field of sport, which is a serious pursuit if one knows where to look and how to discuss what one finds when one is through with the looking.

Wordplay, it must be conceded, often plays a starring role. Hence, Jim had to read about uncorked bats that drove balls into The Champagne.

***

Any ballpark's artificial dimensions constituted limiting conditions for players' natural talents. Even Jim's Olympian came mournfully to appreciate this truism. For example, statistics documented that baseball-champagne interaction happened less frequently at Jim's ballpark than at any comparable venue on the planet. This is *the* pitcher's ballpark, hitters endlessly parroted. Jim felt nauseous when they said such things, although he only occasionally admitted this to himself and never to others.

***

To the consternation of the powers that be, the game's first pitch was delivered at 1:10 p.m. sharp. The owner and the mayor engaged in an unfortunately lengthy disputation before a near-sellout crowd; terrorists from the children's hospital burned orange tracks in the dirt with their powered wheelchairs (led astray, it seemed, by Shriners with infield wanderlust); and before one could say extra commercial block or politely decline a second helping of Seth's and Hector's notoriously predicable *keys of the game*, America's pastime was tardy flipping its we're open for business sign.

***

First pitches, and not only the Little Prince's first pitch, exist in a time/space where bleacher creature and upper-deck proletarian—any spectator not laser-focused on the pitcher-catcher battery—may be unable to confidently distinguish between warm-up and counting pitches. For those paying close attention, however, today's ponderous prelude was worth the wait. The first pitch delivered other than by a contest winner, community volunteer, or returning franchise dignitary; the first pitch issued from an unknown, late-announced surprise starter who didn't warm-up at all; the first *counting pitch* issued by a latter-day Dave Rozema, the team's one and only Rosy; the first pitch sucked the oxygen from the air. Even the Little Prince was breathless. Standing on a tiny raised surface in the middle of Stade de Stefanski, he couldn't have felt more exposed, more alien, more alone.

***

Palmer, though he wasn't Palmer, extended his barely old enough to vote leg. He tantalized as his toe-tip seemed to identify the spot where Venus would appear the next morning. The writerly press box duo on-high saw in him magnificently well-stretched hamstrings and an almost Balanchine aesthetic. Royalty-earning observers seated on the same wavelength envisioned underwear ads of yesteryear and those that might materialize by-and-by. *Weaponized ballerina* fired across one set of synapses, while *synchronized with gravitation* occurred in a parallel universe. Bobs Costas and Uecker simultaneously appreciated the exceptional grace and smooth arc of gravity's rainbow.

Our press box double helix—bookend bookworms known for knotted mixed metaphors and slathering alliteration—did more than merely appreciate and describe. Independently, they resolved that they would not be undone by what they were watching; they would make something of it. Some pause, some gathering of self, was perhaps unavoidable. They even hesitated to glance in the other's direction lest their eyes reveal an unseemly coveting: his bright home whites, his length and fluidity.

A hitch preceded the hurler's bow to the cup. His butcher-block hands were marbled with romaine lettuce creases. Lengthy digits covered the ball in pockmarks. His wind-up—oh, his riveting wind-up—twisted him not unappealingly. Lips and eyes in sync and evidently binocular, he glanced skyward before engaging the box-shaped target. A white orb, he sent into the ether. A regulation baseball into broad televised daylight.

***

Signed. Sealed. Delivered. That's what Mr. Reginald Ross incanted while standing on the sidewalk across from the stadium. Mr. Ross was a newly minted octogenarian watching the game on a hand-held device, a gift from his grandson, Reginald Ross III, or Reggie. Mr. Ross held the screen with outstretched arms and participated in ritual celebration of opening day, as he did every year when he was able. On his own while Reggie was in school, Mr. Ross repeated words he knew from his youth, that he knew from his support for Barack Obama, words that he knew from his mother and from her mother before that, words for good luck, for good luck and prosperity, for good luck, prosperity, and to ward off malignancy against him and his cherished kinfolk.

***

Atwater Addison was a cleat-digging poker player who burrowed into the batter's box. Atwater's penchant for bluffing served as comic relief for his teammates. True to form, he appeared as fearsome as possible, and then, mercurially, went limp to coolly observe the ball's inaugural flight. The confusion that can ensue between here-and-now and televised realities was felt in Atwater's softer tissues, and he used this relatively developed sense and sensibility to analyze the first pitch. Atwater recognized that it was an unbelievably slowly developing breaking ball. It made its way through a shroud of what smelled like sausage smoke that had settled inopportunely, at least for the offense, between mound and plate. Addison's baton stood calmly in relation to these events from its customary although not strictly essential right shoulder resting position, while Atwater's ability to taste ran from his mouth like the fork chasing after the spoon.

***

Whoa, man. Did you see that, Seth. Addison was clearly taking all the way.

***

As luck would have it, the visiting team's leadoff man, Atwater Addison, was clearly taking all the way. Atwater—whose mother named him after Lee Atwater for no reason other than she heard the name and thought it unique—knew that taking the first pitch from an unknown pitcher was the professional approach to the type of at-bat which he was at. His third base coach, Otis Redfield, flashed him the take sign. But Atwater didn't need to be told what he knew from years of experience, not to mention, as a student of the game, from theory. Atwater might have even used the word *theory* had it ever existed in his world, but he knew to take the pitch without recourse to semiology.

The pitch started high and inside. In unthinking reaction, Atwater prepared to adopt a prone position in the batter's box dirt. The ball then curved rudely and with obvious mal intent. Atwater straightened and regarded its course through a grimace, which was his intention in any case except for the grimace. The pitch rolled, rotated, and tucked. Its curvilinear trajectory, as became apparent over time, was to the pitcher's left and the batter's right. The ball seemed destined for the catcher's mitt only if the catcher was skilled enough to press his mitt to his right shoe top, which he did, and in a faux nonchalant manner that was thought to encourage umpires toward desirable outcomes, at least from a defensive point of view. Having conducted a probing interview with the pitch as it clipped his zone, plate umpire, Durwood Nuzzi, was pleased to offer it his recommendation, sans hesitation or qualification. Nuzzi's *strike one* ripped the air.

The catcher sent a parabola to the mound. In and around Mr. S.'s aging ballpark, and within many humans within it, a pretense began to take hold, a notion that there was nothing out of the ordinary about which to take notice. Denial insinuates itself all too easily when spread thin over countless rows and columns. The Fouled Ball Girl, self-identified as such on social media and possessed of a growing following as a result, sat in a team insignia-adorned folding chair down the left field line. Lucy Higgins wasn't the sort to blow bubbles or wear pink. She sat with arms crossed, in judgment of the scene laid out before her. The Fouled Ball Girl was self-conscious about paying scant and at most begrudging attention to the pitcher or his first-pitch success. Others may be enveloped by the humming sameness of moments, but Lucy Higgins hadn't yet made his acquaintance and was thus actively disinterested in his story, his surprise opening day pitcher story, his just how young is he story, his what the heck planet is he from story. Lucy, The Fouled Ball Girl, placed a quarter into a vintage arcade machine, and the batter, Atwater Addison, cycled before returning to a statuesque pose.

***

Writers wrote that *Atwater Addison's attention waned not, his eye waivered not. He faced a leviathan, not an unwieldly behemoth, who stood calmly, not to say confidently.* It was certainly true: Atwater Addison faced a nemesis unlike any other. The veteran ballplayer repeated a ritual of second-hand store obscenities that were audible in both dugouts. The profane celerity regularized his breathing and softened his heart.

Others partially conscious burst onto Iwo Jima's volcanic sands. The loud sun scorched some faces. A few ached from the absence of restorative sleep, the usual province of the maladroit. Most watched as the first pitch tore into Addison's flesh, but others had already begun to sink into melting goo. The porous surface grabbed after reserves of attention and forced legs up and down toward the rally point ahead. Neither frantic nor, it could be said, fully self-controlled, a good many in paid attendance leaned-in against the weight of packs, weapons, and increasingly rubbery legs, advancing into time and falling through space.

***

Mr. S.'s ballpark would change hues as Earth and Sun danced a slow dance over the course of the afternoon. It was as though the materials used in its construction were secretly magnetized to bend astronomical radiation. Those who knew Mr. S. best suspected that he had somehow arranged for astrological interference as well, such that color, heat, and fate would comingle. Whatever its precise origins, the heart of the solar system bathed Mr. S.'s delicate flower in a bright celestial palette, casting the ballpark, and those within it, in heavenly pastiche.

***

The opening day patrons did not know it yet, but they would be witness to something more brilliant than lighting. They didn't know it yet, but they would be released from landing crafts and set striving against fluctuating odds determined by no discernable calculus on our nearly spherical planet. Together and apart, they would struggle toward a woven enemy whose grave torrent might singe their ears or poke holes in their arguments. Clouds on the horizon might hide Mount Suribachi, but the hearty few who saw most clearly knew where they were without need of glimpsing it. The focused wiped their already raining brows and coughed ambient dune. If they could, they held their breath. In hope of a clear shot, they sighted-in the mound.

***

Even the very most distracted—those who had succumbed almost completely to the din—should have noticed something out of the ordinary brewing. It shouldn't have mattered whether they were at the dish, malingering around the infield, or guarding one or another cathedral. It shouldn't have mattered whether they were ensconced in bleached seats, boxed in, or clubbing it; whether they were skybox, dugout, or knees jammed neatly into rows and rows of luxury loge. The Little Prince had penciled in his prison notebook that truth should be true for standing room and wheelchair only. The universal logic of languages, their armies and navies notwithstanding, should impose itself seamlessly across generic sports eateries and cluttered home viewing locations.

***

Sammy's contractually obligated look to the dugout nearly complete—what the press box rendered as *sidereal surveillance of Jim Murry's starry intentions*—today's starting catcher turned his head, and, with a tug of the mask that guarded his large brown eyes, used those river-mud orbs to summon the Little Prince, to ask that he hear him out on what was called for, what was next needed. Sammy put down the sign and Nuzzi jabbed the air. The pitcher of baseballs—a novice signed for a song (and I bet not a Martha and them Vandellas song either, thought Mr. Ross)—nodded, set his right foot, and slowly raised his left thigh to a right angle.

He drew his leg back to nearly forty-five degrees, forming a rough triangle, and leaned hard toward third.

***

Standing on Little Round Top, the Youth appeared to himself as he did in his reflections on *Red Badge of Courage*, as a boy playing a man's game. The Little Prince had long been determined to see himself through the literature he read. At first he had asked questions like, Who would he be if monsters were due on Maple Street. Later, as he grew older and wiser, he graduated to pondering which lad was he on the murderous Isle of Golding. (He suspected that he may be Simon but knew this to be a contradiction: Simon would never think of himself as Simon. Besides, the Little Prince conceded soberly, maybe he was Jack, or, more likely, he was no one at all.) So extended was the Little Prince in this peculiar direction that his slicing fastball might as well have been thrown from between East and West Egg. Apart from the Little Prince's sometimes bewildering metaphors and allusions, it was hard scientific fact that the elliptical geometry of his second pitch would be analyzed later as part of a class at MIT.

***

Jesus. *That* was McGregor. I don't mean to swear, Seth, but he threw that pitch like a right-handed Scotty McGregor.

***

The avian-mammal hybrid on high-ground bent and looked in. Hack writers the pitcher read habitually, habitually wrote such things. They presented *looked in* as though *in* were a place one could perhaps visit, maybe call home. The Little Prince appeared to shrug as he scanned Sammy for information, but Sammy's head drooped, and, in accordance with team policy, tilted to his dugout. Samuel Kenneth Robertson, not originally from West Allis, Wisconsin, had been trained to see and be seen since before he could recall. What's the frequency, Samuel Kenneth, whispered the semi-all-knowing His Highness.

***

From his perspective, Sammy saw his immediate task as decoding meaningful gestures and ignoring several which were meaningful only in their intentional meaninglessness. He had dubbed these signals Jim's flipping hand jive. Sammy thought Jim's Flipping Hand Jive would make a winning name for a restaurant in the Atlanta suburbs. Plenty of free parking in back.

For his part, Sammy knew that he didn't *call the game*, as was said. He related the manager's bidding to the mound by translating one type of sign language into another. His mediating role notwithstanding, the lines of authority were clear, and, as far as he was concerned, inviolate. But Sammy didn't know why Jim, or any manager, didn't signal to the pitcher directly. Pitchers had eyes. They could see signs as well as he could. Was it about the need to shake off a sign. Would it look bad for a pitcher to tell his manager, and to his face, no less, that he'd rather another sign. To Sammy's way of thinking, he and catchers like him resembled multilingual U.N. functionaries whose diplomatic pouches contained oversized mitts to match what, in Sammy's case, his wife joked were his Neanderthal cranium and Cro-Magnon appetite. Sammy loved baseball and he knew life was a gift. He had opinions, but, as the starting catcher, he saw things from various perspectives and strove to bring everyone together around shared goals.

Sammy drooped again, holding his head as though guest of honor at his own beheading. He looked up at the batter, whose perspective was opaque to him. By this time, Atwater was wearing Kareem Abdul-Jabbar sports goggles and a face painted in Tim Duncun Expressionlessism, the latter rendering events according to Hoyle, the former plainly comical. (The best breaking ball and the best fastball I've seen in a lifetime of watching and playing baseball—that's what Atwater, in all candor and humility, would tell reporters after the game.) As Fouled Ball Girl and thousands of on-lookers looked on, Atwater Addison was again ready to play executioner, saber high and firmly gripped. Sammy aligned his spine as if he were valet parking heavily armored law enforcement vehicles at Jim's Flipping Hand Jive. He was a battle-tested personnel carrier, right canon mount indicating fastball down, his left palm shrouded in mystery.

***

It made a certain sense, thought the Little Prince. Expand the zone. Entice batters to swing, not at strikes, but at more difficult to strike non-strikes. The point, after all, was to reduce batters' success probabilities. The point was to disappoint batters, even frustrate them. The standard approach basically hinged on temptation. The pitcher-catcher battery coaxed batters into self-defeating time/space confusion. The strike zone: by all means, let us help you lose track of it. Yet, how often had the Little Prince watched in dismay as 0-balls-and-2-strikes counts preceded four straight balls. It seemed to him that getting ahead, and then *farthest ahead,* was the surest path to pitcher diffidence and eventual walk issuance. This confused reality, he figured, begged the question of what became confused. He thought he may have divined a way out.

Upon further reflection, the Little Prince appended a proviso to his otherwise strict pitching theory: pitch strikes regardless of count *except* after starting 3 balls and 0 strikes, wherein a wise pitcher should see the dish running over with diseased red-and-blue skinned Burmese river toads, deadly poisonous to the touch even when perfectly healthy.

Whether the Little Prince's relentless *pound the zone* pitching philosophy could withstand rigorous examination, much less statistical scrutiny, was anyone's guess. He didn't know it and never would, but Sage One and Sage Two were proponents of strikes too. They couldn't validate their thinking any better than could the Little Prince. What's more, they were infinitely less likely than him to give it a whirl, to experiment in practice. But Sage One and Sage Two were comforted in the shared belief that it was not, in any case, their job to validate. They held that it was the writer's duty to imagine, and to explicate as needed, but never to actualize or validate. He who lusts after valid explanation, they would quip, should regurgitate fortune cookies. Entre nous.

Atwater Addison tried in vain to focus. The Fouled Ball Girl tried to focus. And the game's third pitch, when it came, came from the Bonneville Salt Flats and defied GPS.

***

Check the gun, Seth. Check it. Have we seen this since Nolan Ryan. Read it and weep: 1-0-5 miles per hour. Check the gun, Seth.

That is indeed the reading, Hector.

Addison froze, man. He stood there three straight pitches. He never even *thought* about swinging the bat. This kid has got unbelievable heat, Seth. He's unbelievable.

He came right at him.

He did. Put his foot on the rubber and said, come and get it.

Lively heat down the middle, Hector.

You know it, Seth. Big league. The kid's big league.

Addison was in the dugout before Robertson could....

Absolutely, Seth. He bolted, man. Made a beeline. Beeline and bedazzled.

***

Mrs. S. received the crowd's stirring with practiced indifference. She entered the owner's suite on her own, her mind elsewhere. Were we still warming up; she was often unsure about baseball things. Mrs. S. sat and looked to the playing field. She needed to gauge events through Jim's eyes. She saw Jim draped loosely over the dugout rail. Mrs. S. looked to the mound. VIPs vied for her attention. She looked away, but, while staring at a suit and smiling at it, she said a silent prayer. Moments passed. She stole another glance. The Little Prince stood alone in the middle of her husband's sublimation, sporting an irrational number on his back and exposed to everything her Aleksandar most feared. Mrs. S. felt her neck tighten. She tried to repress the worry she felt when she thought of him. She looked about. Mrs. S. needed distractions like other people needed automobiles. At times like this, when one past trauma pounded on the door to next, and, in league, barged rudely into her present, Mrs. S.'s carefully constructed equanimity waivered. She looked to the playing field. She watched as her boy twisted into the sun. When he reappeared, she noticed that he was shaded.

TWO

The Little Prince was a student. He knew that major league pitchers had pitched twenty-three perfect games, twenty-one since 1900. No hits, walks, or errors. Twenty-seven up, the same number down. Fly balls, groundouts, and foul tips allowed; baserunners not allowed. A game with no baserunners on one or the other side was a perfect game for an immortal pitcher, somewhere. This, the Little Prince learned, was the standard measure of a standard perfect game.

It wasn't only their shared opposition to this definitional neatness that led our illustrious sports writers, Sage One and Sage Two, to contend that the most perfect *perfect game* was not, by this reductionist operationalization, a perfect game at all. Since they had witnessed the game in question and penned similar stories afterward, they put aside competing commercial and professional interests and co-authored a book about what they had together experienced.

The Little Prince had purchased the volume at a used bookstore. The story fascinated him. Sage One and Sage Two, he recalled, began their account in about this way: *Wearing home whites trimmed in blue, Armando Galarraga stood on the mound and faced a talented tribe from Down Under. Over eight breathtaking innings, Armando conducted himself like a train over flat geography. Eight parsimonious innings of standard perfection in the books, Armando Galarraga of Cumaná, Venezuela, tapped, then gently rapped, on the chamber door to baseball pitching transcendence.* For the Little Prince, it read like a children's fable.

But, like many children's fables, this one came with a twist. Armando's lyric poem—what Sage One and Sage Two had dubbed *Perfection Lost*—ended with Armando telling the assembled post-game press: *nobody's perfect*. These are the words that come down through history. They have been verified. Even average first-drafters understood at the time what the authors of *Perfection Lost* would later relentlessly plumb: Armando Galarraga would not truck in irony of either kind. And a devilish turn in the story would do nothing, of course, to diminish the Little Prince's reverence.

Journeyman umpire, Jim Joyce, viewed the post-game replay and admitted that he *kicked*, as he put it, a two-out-top-of-the-ninth-inning call that put a runner on first base, the first of the day. His mind-boggling error—the baserunner wasn't even close—erased, at the last possible moment, Armando's rightful place in sanctioned baseball and sport history. Joyce was in position in one moment and beside himself in the next. It was easy for the Little Prince to empathize with both Joyce and Galarraga. Hasn't everyone has been in Shoeless Joe Jackson's shoes. Who gets off Dred Scott free.

What Armando said in response to this situation was this: *everybody's human*. Two additional words for the Little Prince's homespun liturgy. Armando Galarraga and Jim Joyce embraced. Sans enmity, they shared a greater vision and bonded over a higher raison d'être. They were latter-day Socrates and Plato, agreed sports writers for rival *Free Press* and *News*, now bestselling co-authors with few regrets, and, they were glad to share with colleagues, few remainders too.

For his part, the Little Prince dwelled incessantly on the story's coda. Armando's story, indeed, had a coda, which, according to Sage One and Sage Two at least, resolved the tragedy, if perhaps imperfectly: General Motors presented poor Armando with a good-sport(s) car. This act, as well as the pun, sullied an otherwise sacred moment and warranted heartfelt rebuke: multiple broadsides, every broadsheet on deck. Critiques were issued, including from competing hometown newspapers dependent on auto industry largesse. These were echoed more faintly in a co-authored book suitable for children and coffee tables. In time's healing way, many came to feel that Armando benefitted from the egregious corporate obscenity long after the cheering and back-slapping died out, and long after *Perfection Lost* was lost to most memories. What was good for Armando may have been good for General Motors and vice versa. And, in the end, who but out of touch royalty would question that.

***

Long before Mrs. S. had elevated his prospects, and before Armando had inspired his pride, the Little Prince surmised a more perfect perfection, an unimaginable perfection except in his mind's eye. Not Armando's twenty-*eight* batters out, not Fernando's romance with the City of Angels, not Doug Fister's nine consecutive strikeouts; not any who had ever played the game at its highest or probably any level, had pitched more than a few innings without giving up some number of foul balls.

In baseball parlance, never had a game transpired wherein batters failed to lay wood on a pitch, tan some hide, square one up, or crucify oneself in one or another leg, ankle, or foot. Foul balls were as much part of the game as balls that find mitts or clear walls. Foul balls were incomplete forward passes, missed three-pointers, shots on goal.

The Little Prince knew that baseball had never seen a Kim Jong-Un round of golf or a Looney Tune escapade with pitches making circles in the air before heading in reverse and laughing at their pursuers. There was no Edwin Moses, no Nadia, no single-bullet theories. Baseball levels. A hitter who hits safely one-third of the time shines like a star; a team that wins six of ten games is booked for post-season space travel; starting pitchers earn microwaved in-flight meals for five measly lukewarm innings (a lead unnecessary). Embedded in its rules and soaked in its ways, baseball brings stars down to earth.

It was cliché, the Little Prince granted, that infinitely more than twenty-seven at-bats might occur during a game. The rules permitted without encouraging it. Three batters were *scheduled* to bat per inning, but any number could. Catchers might, for example, badly misplay third strikes and allow batters safe islands at first, a scenario that can repeat endlessly. A manager might substitute in the middle of an at-bat, for injury or inclination or what have you. But the leading source of infinity in baseball resided squarely in the fact that teams at-bat face the possibility of unending success: infinite walks, hits, hit-batsman, foul balls, wild pitches and passed balls. A perfectly imperfect pitcher is therefore a clear and present danger to time, although never had an actual line-up fared so poorly as to fail to foul a good number of offerings. The Little Prince conducted research: the U.S. professional average was forty-five fouls per game. To pitch a no-foul game would require elimination of something that happens forty-five times on average per game, from forty-five to zero, in theoretically infinite seconds.

In no one's living memory, nor anywhere in the voluminous historical record the Little Prince studied, was there nary a word of even an all-misses near-miss. Addie Joss threw seventy-four pitches in his perfect game, and Armando's would have been eighty-three. Twenty-seven batters, three per inning, facing three pitches each over nine innings—sans contact—sums to eighty-one unfettered pitches. If this were to happen—if a pitcher were to toss nine immaculate innings in a row—the boys of summer would spend less time in the sun than bush babies. Impossible. Full stop.

Not to put too fine a point on it, but Trey Whitaker was certain to get a piece of a fastball. Phil Reston would drive something off-speed. Brad Pennington and deep counts used the same e-mail password. When he marched to the sea, as often did, Sherman Lewis saw beach balls, and when he wasn't laying waste to over-inflated offerings, this triple-crown winner saw watermelon ripe for Gallagher's hammer. And then there was Coco Richard (*en français*), who, as everyone knew who knew Coco, struck out less than anyone in baseball named Coco or Richard (pronunciation notwithstanding). This group of sluggers would save time, and thus our world.

If *any* professional hitter of baseballs knew that *any* pitcher was, as they say, *consistently around the plate*, then contact was essentially assured. A batter would square to bunt. There was no guarantee of a bunt staying fair or resulting in a hit, but contact—mere contact, putting the ball in play or fouling it off—was assured. Everyone in the big leagues was in *The Bigs* because they regularly connected bats with pitches. It's a tautology from which no one and no team could escape. It couldn't happen because it couldn't happen.

The Little Prince replayed this perfect perfection. It helped him fall asleep. He watched as batter after batter flailed. Off-speed first, he dreamt, followed by white heat. Inside, outside, up, down. Two-seam, four-seam, split-finger. But it was fantasy. Kerry Wood and Max Scherzer threw twenty strikeouts apiece, not twenty-seven. And there were foul balls. He hadn't counted sheep, but he knew there must have been foul balls.

***

We have entered another world, said Jim to himself and to himself only.

***

Jim watched as baseballs spun past wobbling pins and balanced on razor sharp needles. The Angels amazed as they escaped the inescapable. The first three innings were especially stunning, and not only to Jim. Few Angels seemed inclined to active participation. Maybe they were unsure if the game had begun. Maybe they were still in spring training. Maybe they were scrupulous adherents to the dictum concerning unfamiliar pitchers, biding their time to learn his tricks. Maybe the sun and shadows worked against them or they were just good listeners. Regardless, they went quietly.

The fourth inning turned to the fifth. Some questioned whether Nuzzi's strike zone was aiding the pitcher. Video later showed why the plate umpire and crew chief was not especially challenged that day, for pitches hovered around the plate like the condemned stretching out final meals. It didn't help that the Angels faced a pitcher who wrapped baseballs in the full hijab of his lengthy fingers and who mixed dry martinis with chaotic splashes of nut and fruit. This Little Prince possessed physical talents the likes of which had perhaps never been seen in such effective combination. One was incredible velocity. But there was also a variety of pitches thrown at a variety of angles. It didn't matter what Sammy relayed: his pitcher insisted upon room for interpretation. Movement—wild movement—yet so perfectly did each pitch find the strike zone. Zigzags appeared radio-controlled, each pitch a drone sortie silencing doubters and Angels batters in steadily growing numbers. Angels' skipper, Moisés Saramachi, stood at the dugout entrance and watched as the day's collateral damage paced back and forth in Aleppo's ruins, cast and received looks, and congregated in mumbling clutches.

***

It must be stressed that the Angels contributed to their ignominious demise. Initial at-bats were conducted as a stupefied Dallas secret service detail debating firecrackers versus live rounds. When the curtain rose on second plate appearances, the Angels danced out arm-in-arm performing risqué vaudeville on the good ship *Poseidon*: from listing to capsizing with skirts overhead before anyone could mourn the happy new year that wasn't. As they confessed after the game, the more they hacked, the more they pressed to put the ball in play, to time pitches, to get in a groove, the more they focused their energies on the singular goal of please god surviving the at-bat without humiliation, the more they came to resemble Gong Show reality television contestants armed with fractured broom handles. It was Bud and Lou material. Who's on first. Nobody.

As the fifth passed to the sixth and the sixth to the seventh inning, someone on live television—Hector, perhaps—had the nerve to utter the word-combinations Las Vegas and Black Sox. (To be fair, close-ups revealed recklessness the likes of which had not been seen since Bugsy Siegel.) Combined with textbook-defying breaking balls, governed by the laws of physics as they apply on one of Jupiter's seventy-nine moons, the unnatural natural movement of each unpredictable pitch powered unprecedented perfection through the third go-round of a bewitched and bewildered offensive line-up. What had been unthinkable previously now weighed on most minds.

***

It was between the penultimate and the final frame that widespread recognition began to emerge about what was happening: *pitching*. Savvy pitch selection, command over speed and location, and a weirdly wizened personage that was revealed in bouts of stillness, the way he gratefully received and only occasionally shook off the gift of a sign, an almost frail continence between pitches and innings, and all of this in addition to apparent solemnity in the face of mounting angelic gesticulations and expressed misgivings, to which the pitcher reacted more gracefully than did crew chief Nuzzi, who was finally so displeased with The Angels' agitation that he sent third baseman, Ty Rollins, as well as bench coach, Lorenzo Small, to early eighth inning exits, stage left.

The Little Prince's blend of mental and emotional qualities combined with what some were already imagining as the second coming of The Ryan Express. Such velocity. But there was also deception afoot, the likes of which, thought the *Free Press'* Clemens and the *News'* Twain, hadn't been seen since the last time an Amway promoter writhed in moderately priced snake oil. Would there be blood. Entre nous.

***

We come to the top of the ninth, Hector. Regardless of what transpires, history has been made. Jim Murry handed the ball to a kid out of nowhere and never has a pitcher been so dominant. And for the Angels, I guess it's a day that will live in infamy.

You are so right, Seth. We're in Neverland, my man. I'm Dizzy Dean.

Angels have come to the plate and methodically returned to the dugout, one after the other. No one has seen anything like it.

It's humiliating. Have we seen even a fouled ball. I can't remember a foul ball.

No, we've checked. Not a single Angels batter has made contact, other than one pitch we think was fouled into Robertson's mitt for a third strike. That's being examined.

It might have been tipped.

Did you mean to say humbling.

No fouls. Man, I can't wrap my mind around that one, Seth.

Well, they haven't swung many bats, either. We've seen a lot of stunned looks.

It's true, it's true. Deer. I've never seen anything like this. I called my wife.

If you're just tuning in—and we have interrupted other games—the Angels have been mowed down today and with them baseball record books. No hits, no walks, no errors, and possibly no contact whatsoever.

Unprecedented, man. I've said it. I predicted this.

The bottom of the order is due up, Hector, and, it goes without saying, they're all 0-for-2 today and batting .000 on the year. What should be their approach.

I don't know. I don't know. Maybe they should pull a page from Norm Cash and go up there with a table leg. I don't know. You got to swing, though. That's one thing. You *got* to swing. Does you no good to stand there with the bat on your shoulder.

Close your....

Yeah, exactly. Close your eyes and swing, man.

Great for us, though.

Right, sure. I mean, it's great for us. But the Angels have been shown-up, Seth.

***

Mrs. S. was so disinterested in baseball that even at this momentous moment she was thinking about a recent holiday when she took her Little Prince to Florida for what she said was going to be work with a noted pitching coach but which turned out to be extended time in Key West and a house full of six-toed cats. Other things happened during that trip upon which she did not care to dwell. There was an altercation right on Worth Avenue and another incident that involved what Orlando Police called pure grain alcohol. Mrs. S. loved her ward of the court, who she envisioned as noble and upright. But from that trip forward, she realized that she did not, and would probably never, fully or truly understand her little prince. She would not countenance his every decision nor accept his every thought and position. There was a part of her prince drawn to win-or-die sentiments. He could be reckless. He knew little, she feared, of facts, business, and life. He courted risk, tempted fate. He liked Hemingway, London, someone known as David Foster Wallace.

***

If he gets into any kind of trouble, and I mean if he's crossing a parking lot and we see a car backing out, we're bringing in Sanchey.

Okay.

I don't think he's going to, but just in case.

Do you want me to call the bullpen.

No, I don't want anyone up. What if he saw that.

Okay.

It's merely two runs.

Right.

I've seen guys blow no-hitters and lose a hundred times.

Right.

Just want to be ready.

I know.

Have you seen anything like this, Jeff.

You know no one has seen anything like this.

I've been in baseball for 42 years.

I know.

Look at him: a cool cucumber. Sitting down there.

Looks it.

A Say Hey Kid with headphones.

Never seen nothing like it.

Right. Who's up.

Gupp.

Gupp. Jeff, I'm telling you, you can't make this stuff up. He's a fastball guy.

He is. The scouting report says he's a low-ball pull-hitter.

Jeff, get Sammy over here. And please make sure Sanchez is awake out there.

SAY HEY LITTLE PRINCE

***

Moisés Saramachi had guided The Angels through five campaigns. Not a single losing season and three postseason appearances made him a lock to extend and perhaps expand upon his lucrative contract. He and his agent had a game plan. A former catcher turned manager, Moisés was hired to rebuild a team that had as many baseball woes as it had financial woes. He surprised the fanbase when his Angels secured the second wild card in his first year at the helm. That they succumbed—his favorite word in English—that they *succumbed* in the divisional series in three straight games to the Yankees cost him nothing. His WAR was evident. His mail was delivered to the clubhouse. He was twice third in league manager of the year balloting.

Saramachi stood like he usually did, near the dugout's entrance, a field combine showering passersby in seed particle while watching history in the making. It occurred to Moisés that maybe this history-making was somehow bad for him. An applecart careening off-kilter. Maybe he should *do* something. Maybe *he* should do something. He had to admit that he felt part of the crowd, soaking it up, taking it all in. He ate a kosher frank with a little mustard and ketchup during the seventh inning stretch. Two of his guys were now tossed salad, but he was enjoying a diversity of experience, relishing the onset of another campaign. The weather was certainly *bueno* (no better word in any language), and Moisés Saramachi, a confirmed heliotrope, bent toward the warmth.

Sure, his troops were cannon-fodder today, but where's the fire. It wasn't a crisis. His guys hadn't tripped and fallen over themselves like keystone cops. They hadn't thrown to the wrong bases, missed cut-offs, or sailed a single vessel into Box Seat Bay. They had struck out. That's all they had done. They had struck out swinging and they had struck out looking (quite a few of those), but what was happening was that they were striking out. Big cuts. Swings cut-down, swings short-to-the-ball, swings for the fences and bubble gum card poses. But everyone had, alas, struck out. (Many had been *punched out*, but why salt wounds.) Moisés had struck out more than most during his own playing days. For a time, his nickname was Mofer Ofer. That's just baseball.

Moisés' ace had fared well. There was no doubt about it. One walk and one ball up in the zone, back-to-back. And if it weren't for the short power alley between the line and that indentation in right, the ball would have stayed in the park. At his stadium, it was nothing but a long fly ball. His guy had had a terrific day. The other guy had had an even more terrific day. His guy had a few walks, one hit-batsman, a wild pitch that should have been ruled a passed ball, but otherwise good command, and except for the walk and bloop-dinger in the third, the game would be tied. The Angels had played decently, and they were still clearly very much in it. Two runs would change everything.

Moisés dug deep inside but could not fully convince himself of his own reasoning. Nor could he rid himself of the gnawing feeling that he would somehow be held *accountable*, his second favorite word in English. He liked to hold players accountable. Might he be held accountable as well. Might he be held accountable not only for an opening day shutout, but for being decimated, made to appear inept, humiliated. What would it mean to endure a perfect game thrown against them wherein not a single Angels' batter could foul-off a pitch, let alone get a hit or draw a walk. *Nobody is perfect against defending western division champions.* He felt that mouse nibble his cheese. He looked to centerfield and let his mind wander around its Horseshoe Falls. He imagined himself captain of a wayward Maid of the Mist, his vessel suddenly at risk of inundation.

***

Seth, it looks like Gupp's heading back to the dugout.

It appears the Angels will pinch hit for Gupp to start the ninth.

Dump Gupp, I guess. Why not, man. The Angels should bunt, Seth.

Gupp is 0-for-2 today, like everyone.

Futility, man. That's what we've seen. Perfection on one side, sure, but futility from the Angels.

El Zander, the big left-hander, will enter the game and bat for Gupp.

El Zander's a power hitter, alright.

They're probably thinking about matching Kline's homer with one of their own.

Yeah, man, I don't know, Seth. I think I like a contact hitter in this situation. You don't have to get it all back at once. You *can't* get it all back at once. Get someone on. Move him over. Put pressure on the defense. Bunt. I don't understand the strategy here.

Hector, I hear you. But that's why you and I are up here and not down there.

***

Mrs. S. takes a call. She cuts it short. She ponders the implications of what she's beginning to sense from the way the crowd is chanting wild-eyed, from the raised voices in even her collection of owner's skybox suites. She waves away a proposed iced tea.

***

Sammy translates: cutter down and away.

A ninety-one mile per hour cutter down and away. Expected result.

Sammy translates: cutter down and away.

Shake off.

Sammy looks anguished: cutter inside instead.

Swing and near-miss.

Sammy puts one finger down and flicks to his right: fastball in.

Wicked jumping fastball at one-hundred and three miles per hour, down and in.

Horribly late swing. El Zander engages in histrionics. In response, patrician and plebe alike demand that El Zander march to his room and think about his poor attitude.

***

Sammy's eyes made oblique survey of The Skipper, the inestimable seadog. Sammy thought that Jim probably hailed from Annapolis, Maryland. He wasn't sure but had been told that Jim once worked as a mate on a three-mast whaling ship. Sammy couldn't entirely discount the veracity of this story; he had never been to Chesapeake Bay nor was he more than passingly familiar with the main outlines of U.S. history. Sammy's face became an accordion as he looked back and forth between dugout and mound. Finally, Sammy set up for Moss, who'd settled in for his third, and, Moss and everyone else figured, his last at-bat. The pitch painted the outer edge. Called strike, looking. Sammy set up inside. The ball caught the inner edge. Strike two, swinging. Moss emitted a puff of smoke. Sammy hung his head and Moss stood ready to lop it off.

The final speed ball made a pop that surprised even veterans Robertson and Moss. They were in the ninth inning and the radar gun was still tracking fixed wing aircraft slowed only by light headwinds and flapping streamers. Robertson and Moss didn't share much in common in that moment except squeamishness for Jim's penchant for fastballs. Sammy dreamed about his new in-ground pool-and-patio and squeezed his mitt for a measure of relief. Jim observed his so doing before noting that the near-capacity crowd was stammering as much as it was cheering. It sounded to Jim as though the paid attendance were mixing chocolate volcanic sand with heaping bowls of afternoon hypoglycemia, or maybe it was that they were swirling the last drops of over-priced malt in earth-ending cups, many too full of gas and rot to squirm safely on the edges of their respective seats. The last amused Jim Murry of Virginia Beach, Virginia.

***

The final batter emerged from a daydream. Serenity intact, he made his way to the plate. El Zander and Moss gazed on from Ole Johnny Bench. History had finally come to this. No longer in the hole, or on-deck, history was due to meet its maker.

***

Per custom, mum had been the word since around the fifth, when speed-talking second baseman, Ricky Fay, announced boorishly that he, for one, was glad this friggin' kid, whoever he was, played for their team and not someone else's. Premonitions were present after the first several batters, but The Phenom didn't grow warts and boils on his face and hands until the fifth. His small-talk passport, never much in use, was then fully revoked, his eye-contact visa let expire. Superstition reigned. Mrs. S.'s once-a-fortnight travelling companion glanced furtively at Ricky over a towel pressed to his stubbly damp face. Television caught the moment in a still and added a pretentious caption crawl at once clever, confusing, and to others annoying: *history or his-story or both*. Entre nous.

Between today's sun and the absolute requirement that he don a baseball cap—the team's official chapeau, Jeff Millsaps thought he didn't need to specify—between the blazing solar radiation emanating from today's roaring fireball and an uncomfortable and ill-fitting beany designed by NASA to stifle the body's natural cooling system; between innings, when commercials whirred for the television audience while those in Stade de Stefanski paid little attention to the shlock promotions and ubiquitous canned musical fare, aka, the damnable horse-hockey that is meant to overwhelm senses between innings; during this intermission, the home-side pitcher needed an absorbent towel and a few moments of quietude and opportunity to read and listen to a little music, to help take his mind off his ill-feeling toward the combustible lit by the sun's oppressive match.

The subaltern hired hand might have turned the tables on his teammates with self-effacement were it not that all they cared for was the ritual protection of stray albatross. Hey guys, is the silent treatment necessary. If only he could lose the cap, to be liberated from its damp weight. Dearest Jeffery, my kingdom for a cap-free crown.

***

Wilson Huddlescamp, a twelve-year veteran and former two-time gold-glove first-baseman, screwed his feet into the right-handed batter's box and looked down at what he'd done. He was history's last hope, and history's last hope was skinny, bald, and painfully self-aware. His bat— the bat for which he had spent weeks during the off-season searching— was so reedy that it made high-pitched music against a swirling wind like the one that made itself known and which gave every impression of sticking around. On the road, people would mock Hud by yelling *phone home*, so long and pale were his neck and arms, so large and triangular was his expressive pink face.

On this day, and for the first time in his journeyman career, Wilson Huddlescamp had heard himself think that maybe he was indeed an alien, that he no longer belonged among these people, if he ever did, these people who occupied themselves with such a strange and ultimately pointless rite. The alien now faced what was perhaps the most menacing representative of Earth's Human Species, who, it so happened (and in part because of Hud's earlier difficulties at the plate), was one out away from sport immortality. Hud felt as though he might be lost in the moment, that, if he did not catch his breath in his nostrils and empty his mind, he might fall over—timber: he's dead. This had happened. An umpire once dropped dead on live television. Hud was haunted by it.

***

The first pitch not only eluded Hud, which was to be expected, it seemed to affect his affect. As he stood immersed in the wake of the pitch, he reflected on the feeling that his basic sense of life and its several essential elements had been temporarily upended. He watched what he watched, a fastidiously if also prosaically stitched and sewn baseball, but he watched it originate at middle distance from a bygone era. Hud struggled to see the world as it was, much as he sought to suppress the loneliness welling and inspiring disturbing clarity. Was he coming apart. Was his being unsewn.

Will enunciated audibly to himself all four syllables of the words: Luis Tiant. The twist in the windup went so far around as to leave Luis, characteristically, facing Lake Champaign. When he finally uncoiled, the straight change that followed reminded Will of Boeing 747s that had floated over LAX when he was Willie to his mom and Hud to the kids in the park a few blocks over. He remembered being awed by these heavy dancers. How could such cavernous machines float so breathlessly over the Pacific. Were they made of Hawaiian balsa wood. Were their engines made of Portuguese cork. *Spruce Geese* said a precocious elementary school student bound for university study. Maybe, he reckoned, they were in fact aerodynamically experimental kites, a string binding them one to the other and guiding them invisibly toward rendezvous with the overdeveloped *terra firma* that was his sprawling hometown. He smirked at the thought.

Hud had plenty of time to consider the sublimity of the moment while he drew his bat back from what he would later describe as a ghastly, ill-conceived swing, the ball reaching Sammy's glove about the same time as little Willie steadied himself, holding onto the family room couch for support. He looked at the ump, Durwood Nuzzi, alumnus of Oakland Catholic High School in Pittsburgh, Pennsylvania, who was in his own world, a western Pennsylvania world of Fallingwater, Cathedrals of Learning, musty Braddock opium dens, and the avuncular Nuzzi Clan of Parker Circle, all of which fell somewhere in the great middle of the country. Durwood, whose late-mother had been a saint and whose late-father would have been so proud; Durwood was neither shaken nor stirred.

Hud looked away from the crew chief and back toward the mound, to which his gaze now remained fixed even though he was imagining how he was destined to bank gently to the left en route to the dugout and then afterward to the clubhouse. Eventually Hud would retire to the team motor coach that would wind its way to the team hotel, the same past-its-prime high-rise The Angels occasioned when visiting this or any similarly deindustrialized city. Once ensconced in privacy, Hud would locate his dilapidated luxury suite bed, pull the frayed golden rod covers over his tired head until such time that he could no longer and had to admit that he needed to breathe, that he wanted to breathe, but also that he wanted to go home, to lie there in a state of peace, unmoving.

Tim Wakefield was next to make an appearance on the mound. Will watched as the pitcher adopted a casual stretch position and set his feet. Suddenly, there came a knuckleball. Old movie footage flickered of a pitcher patting his hands atop his team insignia-stitched cap, taunting him a second time. Hud consciously refocused. He had seen quite a few knuckleballs in his day and reflected on the fact that Wakefield was one of the best to throw them. The Pac-12 was loaded with knuckleballers when he was in college, and most of them were successful at the collegiate level. Hud thus recognized that which he subsequently studied over the course of its sixty feet, six-inch circuitous sojourn toward Sammy's mitt as a menace unlike any other pitch. The air battered the barely rotating ball, which reacted as a feather or discarded candy wrapper. Hud bent his ears to the ball's bumblebee flight without interference or thought of chase.

***

Sammy also knew knuckleballs, although he was more concerned that he did not recall requesting one. Did Jim Murry sign-off on a knuckleball. Maybe he had missed something. Did he even know the sign for a knuckleball. Could it be that Jim signaled directly to the mound, Sammy out of the loop, and now Sammy would find himself in post-game crosshairs. How do you feel about the passed ball that led to The Angels amazing ninth inning comeback. Do you think your family is safe. Are you planning to commit suicide. Do you plan to leave a note. Are you more apt to type or handwrite it.

Sammy's solar plexus relaxed only when a white, red-flecked *balle papillon* nestled into his still glove, its silk wings laid low from its journey through heat and wind. Hud stood with his rolled newspaper, which he used to kick non-existent dirt from his cleats, one after the other, keeping his eyes forward, his outward countenance steady.

As soon as he saw the abomination leave his pitcher's hand, Jim Murry knew that he had all sorts of problems. He dreaded the microphones, tape-recorders, and videography specialists. Did he call for a knuckleball. Why did he call for a knuckleball. If Jim hadn't called for a knuckleball, why was it that a knuckleball had been thrown.

***

Moisés hung his head, all purple and pink and moist from the day's sun.

The dugout mooed at passing cars and drew comfort from common belief that, regardless of whether Will Huddlescamp would foul a pitch, hit a pop fly, give life to a squibber capable of finding the sanctioned field of play, or, glory be to the creator above, scratch out a base hit, their pay checks were secure with Wells Fargo. They were professionals.

***

The Fouled Ball Girl was the first field-level team representative to break ranks from normative baseball stoicism. Her spontaneous convention floor demonstration was, however, premature. Fouled Ball Girl leapt from her seat, arms raised, and shrieked in such a high-pitched and incomprehensible manner that the principal reaction was half-hearted ear-covering from the nearest, hence wealthiest. No one else seemed to notice nor cared if by chance they did notice. It was strike two. Innumerate Fouled Ball Girl didn't appear to care either. No one would be embarrassed to lose control of one's bowels in a scramble from beach to foxhole. No one would think of making fun of a comrade, whether grunt, quartermaster, or butter-bar: hey, butter-bar, you fouled yourself. Ha. Other than due to combat fatigue, such a thing would not happen.

***

Seth, this is incredible. I shake my head, man. I shake my head.

I am with you, Hector. There are no words. We're witness to something which will never be repeated. I honestly do not know what to say.

I speak three languages and I don't know what to say. Imagine Hector Emmanuel Gonzalez speechless. So unbelievable. I wish my son were here.

You and me both, Hector.

SAY HEY LITTLE PRINCE

***

The third pitch was destined for the pantheon. Gibson against Eck (which displaced Gibson against Goose, the pantheon abiding one defining moment per godhead). Pudge's voodoo. In the pantheon. Hank rounding the bases. In the pantheon. The shot heard 'round the world except in Lexington and Concord. In the pantheon. Sammy might flip his mask and charge the mound. Auditioning for the pantheon.

***

The Little Prince did not care about his place in history; he just wanted to talk with Jim. The Little Prince was weighing when he might inquire with Jim if Auerbach was a hero growing up, and, if he was, why a kid from the Eastern Shore would give a fig about Red Auerbach. As this .22 caliber thought passed through his mind, the Little Prince decided to ignore signs from the dugout, and, the rest of the way, stick close to the Red Sox in whom he had developed a curious degree of trust.

***

His third pitch could be a Rocket fastball or a Pedro change-up. The latter was politically attractive, although he was compelled to acknowledge that he might as well be addicted to the former. What would be singular and true to himself, he asked. This was the third pitch, to the third batter, in the ninth inning of the season's opener: maybe he needed to ride in on Apollo's chariot; maybe he should dissolve into a blistering fireball.

Ambivalence reigned in his unevenly developed interior world. The Little Prince wondered if, in the end, he would be better served by witchcraft than worship of the sun king. This thought intrigued him. He craned his neck. He felt the need to prepare for transition from game to post-game, from the show, as he'd heard others call it, to what he worried would be never-ending interview room purgatory. The Little Prince charted a course from over-exercised sandbox to the still quiet of the night. He knew that Mr. S.'s artificial reality, however intentional in its construction, could not protect him from impending corruption any more than it could sidestep bundles of energy from even long-extinguished stars. The precocious Little Prince had discerned that immanence is the reality that transcends; transcendence is only a reality within us.

He stood on the mound thinking about anything but baseball, it seemed. He might deliver the mail from Patagonia to Timbuktu for all he knew, and, when spent, when thoroughly exhausted, risk death flying reconnaissance sorties in the next war. What was most important, the Little Prince believed, was his responsibility to others. This required no more than that he deliver himself, wherever he was called, fully and on time. It also required, he admitted, that he expect nothing in return. If this weren't excruciating and impossible, the Little Prince thought it might be a good way to live.

***

Mr. S.'s lighthouse went dark at the witching hour. The Little Prince knew this with particular certainty. The Little Prince believed that life experience constituted baptism in truth. He liked to stay up late in order to ponder the blackest time, when stars blanket winter beaches and galaxies taste of raw oyster. But ambient noises interrupted his continuity, perhaps, he guessed, because he no longer, hadn't in a long while, taken for granted his flow. The Little Prince returned to the fact that, whatever was the case philosophically, he had work to do, a project to which he must attend. He thus finally resolved to put aside, at least for the time being, that not usually, not regularly, accessible to the ticket-punched parishioners of Mr. S.'s once awe-inspiring but nowadays quotidian citadel.

The surprise opening day pitcher wrestled with his thinking as seconds became minutes, as he stood in front of hundreds of thousands, maybe millions, of the planet-bound, many who had tuned in to form an electronic bond with this single stitch in time, to witness what they hoped would bring them hope, an antidote to the inevitable grind as they knew and defined it. With Sammy flapping for his attention, the epiphany the Little Prince had fervently sought then arrived, not on a winged chariot, not from the dugout by way of Sammy, but from a pit deep within him: not The Spaceman, he thought. *Not Spaceman Bill Lee.*

***

Sammy was not afraid, per se. Like everyone, he could experience fear, but he was not afraid that a ball would strike him in the faceguard or his off-hand or bounce so far in front of him that he had to protect his nether-regions. He would not, he was sure, need withstand a concussion-inducing blow, nor was it likely that a ball would breach his neck-guard, which dangled, a yam protecting an apple. Sammy was, at times, filled with diffuse anxiety. It lingered down every tunnel and collected at the bottom of every locker within him. It could be painful, a somatic angst experienced as stomach sickness, chest heaviness, and brain-aching distractedness. It shot waves of sickening juice through his body, acting as a kind of low-intensity warfare designed to wear and weather and leave him worn. Nothing had gone as expected today and he chalked that up to the decision, on which he was not consulted, to start a kid who no one knew much of anything about.

They were going to win on opening day. That was always a good omen. Sammy was ready to call his first no-hitter and his first perfect game. He was one strike away, as they all were, from baseball immortality. Sammy knew that his bat didn't have a hit in it which could match this moment. He couldn't throw down to first or erase a baserunner stealing second in a way, in any situation he could imagine, that could hold a candle to this one defining moment. All he had to do was keep his glove in the strike zone and squeeze. The kid hadn't missed all day and Sammy was reasonably sure that he wasn't going to miss now. He took comfort in knowledge that E.T. could swing if he wanted to.

***

The late Dan Quisenberry looked in and prepared to throw a third pitch to the twenty-seventh Angels batter. He looked long, and, Sammy thought, approvingly at the sign. Relevant pairs of feet were set. The game's newest greatest pitcher drew his left leg, but just slightly, and then swung it toward the fountains as they cheered him on. In an elegant short-lived motion, he turned his left shoulder down as he twisted himself up and under to deliver what many knew to be a submarine pitch, a nearly underhanded pitch, his pitching hand but a few inches off the mound at release, something no one could remember Hal Newhouser—Prince Hal—attempting let alone making look easy.

Only a few saw a submarine pitch that would have made softball great, Monica Abbott, proud. A few more may have felt this tension but moved quickly to submerge below surface and avoid detection. Only one press box member had a second thought. He watched the late Dan Quisenberry, as he was wont to do over his All-Star career, direct a baseball at average velocity from an unusually low starting point to intersect the strike zone at the front edge of the plate. Its vector was otherwise pedestrian. With overwhelming feelings of sympathy, the Little Prince looked-in at Will Huddlescamp.

***

Would Hud swing. Would he. Why would he *not* swing. Eighty pitches had caught, or grazed, Nuzzi's strike zone. Even a boot-shook rookie would be in proverbial swing-mode. Back in Sprout League, kids spewed batter, batter. In high school, Hud himself swore allegiance to the flag of Swing the Damn Bat. In college and in the minor leagues, Hud's teams had spiced bat-swinging encouragement with colorful cultural diversity, a kind of baseball profanity smorgasbord, an inclusive world music of smack.

But Hud was shrouded in silence as he watched Dan Quisenberry—*The Quiz*, one of the most decent and humble to ever play the game, a baseball player who in retirement became a published poet before he died at age 45 as a result of brain cancer—Hud watched The Quiz blow an eighty-five mile-per-hour rise pitch past him on the inside half of the plate. The inner half was Hud's favorite part of the plate, as borne out over twelve years of playing the game professionally and with a mountain of data to back what used to be that which he would have thought true by having lived it. Sammy sprang from his crouch, a music box doll cranked to life. A cacophony flooded the playing surface. Sammy looked to his bench for guidance.

***

A profoundly deaf writer hastily composed a headline for his online publication: *Quiz Magic*, it enthused. This same writer's surreptitious lip-reading led him to misunderstand press box references to Monica Abbott as references to his hero, Jim Abbott, the fellow who needed only one hand to excel as a professional pitcher of baseballs. Jim Murry, who admired Jim Abbott, and Moisés Saramachi, who admired Jim Abbott, each clapped as though grasping after something they had won. To Mayor Landry's delight, nearby gunboats raced each other to issue volleys of friendly fire, while around the stadium white whales gave their punch-drunk captains a last wave before drowning them in their seats. A quizzical scribe stood at the back of the press box and quietly, without betraying his method, observed his colleagues' vociferous gestures.

On the field of play, alas, the Little Prince and Hud caught each other's eyes as the former finished a thoroughly unfamiliar pitching motion and the latter stood motionless at the plate. *He almost fell,* they thought. It was commonplace confusion of subject and object to which each had accommodated themselves. The work nearly concluded for the day, he believed, the Little Prince started for home, eyes cast down, his arms hanging unsteadily at his pulsing sides. For this part, Hud turned left to fulfill his known destiny.

THREE

Jim's was the league's most impressive office. Having largely avoided the unavoidable work of scouting during his meteoric post-playing days rise through the managerial farm system—thus having avoided travel to Japan, and, for that matter, journeys to other distant nations where soil quality and local climes nurtured baseball players from shoots bursting with exceptional strike-out and home-run potential—Jim's forensic knowledge of his rivals' managerial digs was limited to U.S. and Canadian house calls. This included the senior circuit, which, by definition, appeared on his schedule intermittently if ever. In this way and over many years, Jim developed a fund of comprehensive comparative data and a league-wide reputation for endearing vanity.

Scouting, Jim knew, meant long nights in mirthless standardized hotel rooms, and if Jim knew anything without need of firsthand experience, it was that he hated to be alone and that he loathed standardized anything. His anti-scouting antics conspired over time with bouts of random luck (once an earthquake saved him from a two-week trip to Nicaragua, another time an outbreak of flu kept him from a month-long swing through Mexico), the ultimate result being that Jim was spared opportunity to languish, smoke swirling skyward, in The Hiroshima Toyo Carp's suite of elegant rice paper manager's and manager's assistant's offices, so large and well-designed that smoking was permitted throughout, so proportioned and well-appointed that team ownership, at the insistence of the Prime Minister's protocol adviser, used the space to host Bush 43.

Earl Stefanski was not content to let The Carp have all the bragging rights. Margie's younger brother shared with anyone who had to listen, and, in addition, with Jim once a month on average, a mental slide deck about Rice University, Earl the Pearl's alma mater and a significant source of his identity and amusement. One oft-repeated story concerned Rice's donor-funded baseball stadium, which, in its sanctum sanctorum, harbored a magnificent oval-shaped manager's office. Jim had never visited his counterpart's digs, but he imagined it as whitewashed in laundered petrodollars.

Jim's mind's eye saw nouveau dude ranch décor and gold Kuwaiti bathroom appointments raising up cripples, lepers, and floor-to-ceiling crystal trophy cases. He imagined bronzed bases commemorating trips to Omaha past and a diamond-encrusted a 3-D replica of Houston's Star of Africa, his secret code for the towering monstrosity.

Jim conjured a fiery middle-aged Billy Graham at the edifice-blessing ceremony. In his divining, neither the Right Reverend nor Rice could resist darkening their door with presidential eloquence. Jim envisioned the speech recorded on parchment in a slightly rounded Dedication Day display, near a lighted portrait of Big Train Jim Asbell.

Earl Stefanski didn't seem to register Jim's speculative analysis. Earl continued to lend and lease luxury suites and entertained guests in them as only The Pearl could. As Rice's stadium settled into its shifting mixture of sandy soil and dark gumbo clay, Owls Baseball, without fair warning, went from championship caliber to basement dweller. Three losing seasons in a row lit a fire under an otherwise conservative university administration but were welcome kompromat for Jim vis-à-vis Earl. Per collegiate athletics SOP, Rice dispatched its manager with a golden parachute of deferred compensation and began cultivating its way out of its rounders rut one five-star philanthropic gift at a time.

An alumnus of Rice's accelerated three-year turf management program with a minor in cultural anthropology, Earl would say of himself that he was a cut above, that he was a cultural universal. Jim found it hard to see himself in Earl, but, reasoning that he uttered a few tall tales himself; that peace with Mrs. S. was worth two in the bush, that anything beat analyzing infield specifications with The Pearl, Jim tried to keep his oil and gas in the ground.

***

Manager Jim Murry shut the door to his office behind him, tossed his cap on his custom-made four-person leather sofa, ignored the non-stop buzzing of his phone, and went straight to the unending mahogany bookshelf that lined the wall behind his desk. It didn't take Jim a moment's reflection, however, to conclude that there was no time for the sort of nuanced documentary and archival research that he had had in mind since the sixth inning on. He estimated that he had four minutes before he was expected in front of the press, and time being time, those minutes would be experienced as glorified seconds.

Jim lit an English Oval and foresaw a clamoring conclave in its smoke. He would have to be himself, he figured. He would have to tell the world that he was probably as awed as them, that he was as unnerved as they were, if anything, maybe more so.

But today's pitcher, Jim concluded quickly, would need care and feeding. As far as Jim knew, his surprise starter turned baseball wunderkind lacked meaningful fourth estate experience. He was eighteen; he certainly hadn't appeared on *Nightline*. This kid might not understand that the questions would likely begin deceptively, like smiling wiseguys maneuvering for an easy kill-shot. It wouldn't take long before a dock's worth of stevedores would openly draw their hooks, wedging them into perceived cracks, jostling for leverage. Jim's mind wandered through the Roman Senate to a scene in Kipling that he had stumbled across recently in its John Huston adaptation. He allowed his ears to hear cloying questions as crabs slapping at each other's claws, a struggle to be the first to affect an iron hold. His boy was in danger, alright. Jim predicted that they'd come at him via celebration of his incredible natural raw talent.

***

A knock at the door wired Jim's glass jaw. He wheeled around to see the Little Prince genuflecting under the doorway blinds, Jim's homage to film noir. Jim was immediately incensed by the earbuds. Jim's sanctuary muffled uproarious shouts of joy, but he could still hear Sammy whooping it up, and he could still see Bunchie covered in infield from head to toe, fists pumping like a toddler greeting a morning filled with wonder and opportunity. Jim could see Kline deep in conversation with a local television reporter who probably couldn't care less about his game-winning drive, and he observed Ricky Fay, all those words pent-up for four, maybe five, long innings, but now, thanks to Ricky's lungs, ricocheting off lockers and refreshment tables and freshly rubbed leather seating for the players' exclusive enjoyment. Did Mrs. S.'s darling Little Prince, this most rank rookie of all rookies, mean to ignore all that. Was this kid *that* unaware of his surroundings. Or, was he just too good for his teammates.

***

Umm.

Come in here and close the door, I need to talk with you.

Listen, Jim. I can't....

Are those things on.

No.

Well, then take them out, would you.

Yeah, sure. Jim, I need to head out.

Son, what we need to do is to talk about the press conference.

No, I'm heading out because....

The press is going to ask you a lot of questions because of what you did this afternoon. If I were you, I would keep your answers.... What did you say.

I'm heading out. I'll change at home. We can talk tomorrow.

Look, kid, I appreciate that you're new to all this, but you are required to talk to the press. You understand. You are required to come to team meetings, too, by the way. Heck, the trainers are going to want to talk to you, I'm going to want to talk with you, a lot of people are going to need to talk with you.

Yeah, but I have to go. Let's talk tomorrow.

Dave is going to want to talk with you. I assume Mrs. Stefanski is going to want a few minutes. Photos and all that. You do realize that you made history out there.

I don't know. It depends on what you mean by...out there. Jim, I have to go.

***

An uptick in the din followed the Little Prince as he made his way through the clubhouse, the normal cacophony reinstated only once he left out the back. Most thought he was readying for the interview room; that perhaps there were out of the ordinary preparations to be made, that perhaps he had something in his car that he needed, or more likely family members to greet, before he then returned for his media victory lap. No one thought he was bugging out, but out he had most certainly bugged.

Although motivations are always complicated, it could be said that the Little Prince was driven from the clubhouse by and for loneliness. His kind of loneliness, the kind that could kill you, made it hard for him to be the center of attention, to play any meaningfully false role prominently. In the Little Prince's experience, which he regarded highly, in which he placed a great deal of stock, loneliness was experienced most intensely, and most satisfyingly, when one was completely and thoroughly alone, when the deadly poison that loneliness is, is free to well up and take hold. There is comfort in its embrace. It adds if one can observe, from a safe distance, an outstretched congregation of alligator arms.

***

Jim stepped back into his office and closed the door. He recalled what Tim McCarver, a catcher like himself, had once said: McCarver reported (as though it were common knowledge), that baseball is a team sport played by individuals. That is, ballplayers are in it for themselves. They maximize their batting averages, make plays, pad stats, and revel in accolades. When he said this, baseball spat its collective chew.

Jim recalled that McCarver's apostasy had emerged during his color-analysis for a major broadcast network broadcast of a major league game. It didn't matter which game it was, but Jim thought it involved the Cardinals. Under immediate assault from an aghast long-time play-by-play sidekick—*recant and beg forgiveness odious maggot*—McCarver conceded that pitchers and catchers might form a bond, something of a duet; might. McCarver's impromptu grand inquisitor couldn't imagine a Baseball Great trashing the sport that every American loved. What about double-play combinations, such as lore's Tinker, Evers, and Chance. What about guys who marry other guy's sisters and wives. What about that, Timmy. *Contemptible mutant scum.*

Given that not he nor another member of the organization had wrapped arms around their conquering hero and pulled him back from whatever escape he sought, Jim felt that baseball's Young Bucks owed its Old McCarvers an acknowledgement. Jim's surprise opening day starting pitcher had won safe passage with a string of at-a-boys and head-pats from men barely old enough to have children, although many of them did. Jim recalled that Larry Herndon had done something similar after a World Series game in which he hit a decisive home run. A private man, Larry claimed his disappearing act was meant to preserve the spotlight for the game's true hero, the starting pitcher, the team's ace. When, in the press room, de facto Mad Men would inevitably demand satisfaction, Jim imagined kneeling to carefully rest Larry Herndon on Fleet Street.

***

Mrs. S. did not know nor care much about baseball. This was well-known. Her husband died. He had bought a majority stake in the team with crazy profits from his statewide network of auto dealerships, including the massive Stefanski Auto Mall not far from the stadium. Mrs. S. inherited the team. Margie—as she was known to the world but who Jim always addressed as Mrs. Stefanski or Mrs. S.—hired a general manager who was to know baseball in her stead and live within her single master rule: turn a profit, don't embarrass me. The general manager who eventually landed the job did so because during his second interview he had the temerity to point out that Mrs. S.'s master edict really contained two rules, to which Margie informed her new G.M. that, to Margaret L. Stefanski, losing money was the greatest of all possible embarrassments.

***

Dave Shoal had assembled a veteran team. He would counsel Jim that *veteran* is not tantamount to high-priced. Dave's kind of veteran was a journeyman. Dave's guiding principle was that multi-year multi-million contracts left G.M.'s with their hands tied. Better to field a team with men who knew the game and had a few years left in the tank, but who hadn't, at least hadn't yet, earned too many brass rings or rang a whole lot of expensive golden bells. He would tell his players, or Jim's players, that working together meant that success could be shared by all. If everyone did their job, if everyone pulled together, Dave would say, if everyone followed the game plan, then everyone together could enjoy success. When Dave spoke of success, it was well appreciated that he meant fielding a semi-competitive, semi-entertaining professional team while assuring a profit for Margie. If things turned out competitive and entertaining, so much more the merry, so much greater the profit. But first things first: manage the payroll.

***

Hector, let me ask you a question.

Fire away, man. But I'm speechless. I'm exhausted.

Can we expect this to be repeated. Will this kid be forever unhittable.

No, man, there's no way. Hitters are going to be ready for him next time. They have tape to watch. They're not going to stand there for three innings like the Angels did. No, we're going to see some guys making contact, some hits and runs. It's the nature of the game. He's just human.

I tend to agree with you, Hector, but it occurs to me that we don't know his ceiling.

He has huge ups, no questions. Raise the roof, Seth.

Can you imagine the attention that will be paid to his next outing. Presumably he'll next start against the White Sox when they come in next week.

You can count on it, Seth. But to go back to your last question, they'll be ready. Those hitters will be playing for hitters everywhere, you know.

But hopefully we'll win.

Oh, yeah. I mean, sure. We want to win. And you know our guys will have a lot of confidence going into that game. We've got this series with

SAY HEY LITTLE PRINCE

The Angels to finish and then the Sox come to town. Got to take 'em one at a time, Seth. But we're off to an amazing start. It's incredible. I mean, our ace is up next. Gotta feel good about that.

***

Akihiko Sato had lived in the United States for ten years, exactly one-third of his life. He recalled fondly his first year in Seattle, which felt so much more like home than the half-dozen other cities, mostly in the East and Midwest, in which he had lived since. Home was Tokyo. It would always be Tokyo. Many Americans seemed surprised when they asked where in Japan he was from. They expected he would be from someplace perhaps they had heard of or more likely someplace unknown to them entirely, not the one city they knew with ninety- to ninety-five percent certainty existed in Japan. And when Akihiko said he was from Tokyo, he meant Tokyo, not some hamlet fifty miles from Tokyo. Americans always told him that they were from Los Angeles or New York, when in fact they were from San Bernardino and the suburbs of Buffalo. Why do you not say that you are from Tonawanda. Why do you disrespect your birth and upbringing.

Akihiko Sato was in fact from Asakusa, a spiritual and long-established Tokyo neighborhood in which his father and mother owned a shop that his father's parents had owned before them and that sold anagogic wares and religious accoutrements, mainly for visitors from the world over but with a sizable local (and older) customer base as well. Akihiko was his parents' only child, but he had many grandparents and aunts and uncles who patronized the family business. A talented student (and web-designer for his parents' online store), this tall and thick and powerful still-growing young man was even more talented in amateur sport than he was as a student at his renowned international academy. In addition to baseball and applied mathematics, Akihiko was a rated fútbol player who seriously considered mid-fielding his way through life. He could handle himself on volleyball and basketball courts as well, and many a coach and college admissions counselor entreated him and his parents to consider all their options.

One day when he was sixteen and sitting in the shop office reading about the firebombing during World War Two, Akihiko decided that he would pursue a career in baseball ahead of other possibilities. From that dedication forward, Akihiko was on course to immigrate to the United States, where he would quickly earn a small fortune.

***

Sammy saw Dave enter the clubhouse. He wanted to hug someone. He was feeling that he should hug Dave and everyone equally. But there were so many people between him and the general manager. And it might appear that Sammy was trying to compensate for his not having hugged the kid, or even much-greeted the Phenom, after his shocking feat. Catchers are supposed to be there for their pitchers. They guide them. They frame pitches, call pitches, they keep the umpire focused on what all-important catcher-pitcher batteries are trying to do. Sammy knew this. He was a veteran. He had caught some of the best and, alas, he had caught some of the worst.

But what had happened today had Sammy feeling out of sorts. Even in the clubhouse, he felt surveilled and indentured, the behind-the-scenes a scene itself. Some guys were acting as if they had won the World Series. Others couldn't shower and dress fast enough. Ricky looked like a guy on something illicit. Sammy glimpsed Jim as he poured himself into his beautiful office like fine wine into an heirloom decanter, but had Jim remained there or had he decamped to the interview room.

***

Team publicist Walker Evans Stefanski, a recent Vanderbilt graduate and Margie's nephew, was also looking for Jim. Walker searched clubhouse nooks and training room crannies, sniffing surfaces like a bloodhound in search of its quarry. Jim was five and by some estimations ten minutes late for the post-game press scrum. While some delay was acceptable— indeed, given the stupendous nature of the game, while some pregnant delay was to be expected and was perhaps even advantageous to Walker's vision for a defining moment in history—Jim's on-going unknown whereabouts was, Walker felt, potentially embarrassing to the team and Aunt Margie. Scooter Libby, as Jim dubbed him, was vexed as well as perplexed, as Jim's scent was everywhere.

For his part, Jim was on the trail of baseball's latest wonder, the fellow who had, as it is said, left the building. Jim stood in the parking lot struggling to recall the make and model of the jalopy in which he'd first appeared, the day when Dave and he were introduced to Margie's brainchild. Jim thought it might have been a Toyota or Honda, but what wasn't or hadn't once been a Toyota or a Honda. He thought it was red, but nothing here bore resemblance to blood. Black and white dominated. Trucks and SUVs.

As he registered the last observation, Sanchez—Jim's closer, his ninth inning money—darted past on a direct line to his vehicle. Jim presumed that Sanchey was headed to his notoriously palatial suburban estate. Evidently, Sanchez had no interest in celebrating today's World Series victory. This may have been because, Jim thought, Sanchez was the single player on Dave's veteran-laden roster who had actually played for a World Series champion. Played for, not played in. Ruben Miguel Sanchez did not see action in the four-game sweep. He was a long reliever then, in a series in which his team had no need of long relief. Sanchez watched as the Giants' starting rotation dominated a Twins line-up that was thought and then proven out of its depth. According to *The Sporting News*, known for its absurd style of writing, the Twins' disappearing act was as surprising as that of a planted volunteer at a magic show.

Jim understood that baseball at the professional level could make kittens out of cats. He meowed but Sanchez was closing the door of his polished red Tesla, and, in any case, was disinclined to acknowledge Jim's presence. Jim stood for a moment and watched Sanchez speed from the parking area. He again surveyed the lot. All black and white trucks and SUVs, except for one candy-ass liquid hydrogen rocket, he concluded.

***

Dave swept into the briefing room and sat behind the Beatles-land-in-America-via-BOAC microphone bank. A logo-emblazoned microphone obscured his clean-shaven cleft chin and sunny disposition. A confident G.M. eventually invited questions.

Why do you hate Christianity.

All I said was that we were bigger than Jesus Christ, that's all.

Why do you think you're gods.

I didn't say we were gods. I said that we are concerned by the madness that seems to follow us wherever we go. We say woo and kids fart the Union Jack. It's like we're shamans. If we were to order our fans to invade an already beleaguered war-torn agrarian country and burn their villages, they would. You know it, we know it.

Well, we love your music and you fascinate us, but we feel that you probably need to be stamped out. Do you feel that you should be stamped out. Would it help if mobs ritualistically burned encoded vinyl conveyance of your wildly popular music.

No, it would not help. Stamping people out is not good. How would you like it if we stamped you out. This ain't easy for us, mates. That's all we're saying. The war is over if you want it to be. The war—*the war*—is over if you want it to be. Let that sink in.

SAY HEY LITTLE PRINCE

***

Jim's pitching coach was also looking for him. Jefferson Thomas Millsaps, Jeff to all, was in search of an infusion of nicotine to anesthetize his many existing as well as expanding variety of tics and jitters. Jeff's hole-in-the-wall was on the other side of the clubhouse from Jim's. It was ashtray and butt central and Jeff's tar-stained skin was occasionally mistaken for sickle cell. A Mississippi native and Ole Miss graduate, Jeff had been a starting pitcher in this day. He had two quality pitches and two secondaries that he'd flip as needed. Having first met as opposing minor league managers, he and Jim had teamed for over two decades. A lefthander, Jeff was more than happy to be Jim's right hand, his loyal second-in-command. Jim didn't need a bench coach because when Jim was tossed, which occurred rarely, Jeff would finish the game with not a curl out of place. Jeff was intuitive, supportive, and steady. He was olive to Jim's canola.

As solid as he was, Jeff was unnerved by this thing with the kid. Jim shouldn't have had to start an unknown rookie. Even though the kid was a true Phenom (and Jeff knew this well before this afternoon's miracle), it was still a risk to start him under such intense conditions. It made Jim and him look bad to the other players, if not also, a tertiary concern, to their managerial brethren. Neither had Jeff relished telling Akihiko that he wasn't getting the ball. Jeff knew Akihiko to be a man who was sensitive to perceived slights and this was, arguably, an actual slight. But Akihiko Sato epitomized quiet dignity and checked any fluctuation in his emotions. Now it was Jeff's turn to check his emotions. Jeff wondered what his coaching brethren would think. Was Jeff doing the right thing. He bent slightly at the thought of facing icy judgment at baseball's annual winter meetings.

***

One might expect renowned sports writers such as Sage One and Sage Two to command front row seating at post-game news conferences, but true sages do not seek the limelight, they do not shout at Mark Antony. It is best not to associate oneself with such ruckus. A writerly writer might instead watch the feed from afar in case there were nuggets to be gleaned, but otherwise, if one still had questions, it was best to pose them one-on-one in the quiet and comfort of Jim's inviting office. This required taking turns, but as turn-taking was a long-acknowledged civic virtue, turns would be gladly taken.

Today, however, Sage One and Sage Two stood in the back of the press room wondering like everyone else what was taking Jim so long to get the kid dressed and in front of an increasingly deadline-adverse mob. Gold Rolex stood at attention, his back to a wall, while Silver Shinola stood at ease. Both writers anticipated that a bejeweled story was imminent, perhaps the keystone of a new book. Each, in fact, was already at work on their respective filigree.

***

The car door swung open and Lucy's mom smiled her into its warm interior.

What a game, huh.

Oh, mom, did you see what I did.

No, dear, what did you do.

I jumped up when I thought the game was over, but it wasn't. Everyone saw me.

Oh, they were probably watching that boy, love. He was something, wasn't he.

Mom, I'm right there in front of thousands of people, and there I am screaming my fool head off after the second strike.

I know, but everyone makes mistakes.

I sat down and pretended like nothing happened.

That's what a lot of people do, dear.

***

The feeling that came over him was unsettling as well as all too familiar. There he was, scrunched low behind the wheel, fully in command of his fire-engine red 1996 Toyota Camry. The Little Prince was parked at about the tenth fast-food restaurant on the right side of the road that he had encountered as he otherwise took random flight from the player's lot several miles back. A half-eaten Warren Burger sat next to him and a Dr. Pepper without ice occupied a broken but still-functional cup holder. He had been engrossed in re-reading a few passages from *Of Mice and Men*, the same few that he had gone over during the later innings of today's game. But now he had lost interest and was once again staring into a weed-infested lot adjacent to High Court Burgers & Fries Store #13. The Little Prince cataloged one tan refrigerator circa 1975, one green electric stove-top oven of similar vintage, and a white enamel washer and dryer set with their respective door and lid wide open. If it were midnight instead of early evening, a waddling raccoon would have emerged from out from the washer or the dyer, it was anyone's guess which. The Little Prince deployed his tongue in a game attempt to free a piece of French fry lodged between shaky molars. He coughed. And then came tears.

***

Depression is pain. People say that depression is sadness, but sadness is sadness and depression is pain. The challenge, from a literary perspective, was to describe the pain, because the thing about all pain, whatever its type—whether measured with smiley and not-so-smiley face icons at doctor's offices, measured by CIA operatives at work in faceless prisons, measured by research faculty at publicly defunded state universities, wherever, whatever—the thing about pain is that it is the thing in the world that is most not like language, the thing least legible on planet Earth.

Pain is not symbolic. If there's a needle in one's eyeball or if rats are eating one's face, then there are no adequate words, no etchings and scribbles or sounds that can capture the terror and horror that are principal constituent elements of the dying that one is doing. Not living one's dying, but dying one's dying. Living in pain, dying in pain.

Depression-pain, for all its elusiveness, and, in fact, probably because of its elusiveness, is more dangerous than extra-legal rendition or totalitarian state pain, which at least has the apparent benefit of dumb, brute transparency. Depression-pain hides itself from itself; it refuses location. It emerges from blood cells and connecting tissues and cartilage, leaving bones and muscles, and, as often as not, radiant smiles, intact. It's everywhere and nowhere simultaneously, impossible to withstand but also, at other times, a cloak brushed off against a waiting hook. Depression is the biomedical pain that results from the internalization of everything that is unacceptable, in this and all known worlds. Depression-pain is context-awareness run amok, the price paid for the classic tradition in sociology, for Auguste Comte's hubris. On this he sat and thought.

The thin book still in his hands, the Little Prince recalled that it wasn't Steinbeck but Styron who once described a moment when he, William Styron, was being driven through Paris streets at night; where he, Styron—an accomplished writer, a man of learning and letters and the recipient of accolades and honors (in fact, it was an accolade of some kind, an honor of some sort, which led him to Paris)—where Styron realized that, because of the sort of pain that depression is, that he,

William Styron, might not survive his depression. Mrs. S.'s royal heir, the progenitor of this thinking, had requested Styron information and received it instantaneously from a world-embracing search engine accessed via a hand-held kept safe at his side even while pitching.

The Little Prince searched the wreckage before him as he shook himself gently. He'd better go, he said. He repeated it, this time aloud. *I had better go.* His insides started to object to the recently masticated food products, and his ears continued to ring from what he had recently lived through. *I had better go.* When he said it, it came out garbled and non-committal. *I had better go.* He twisted himself, muscles bulging, his face wet. Start the car. Check the mirrors. Earbuds, gears, accelerate through space.

FOUR

Jim's secret office entrance was known to him and Jeff and not more than twenty additional confidants. In-the-knows excluded Mrs. S. and Dave but included *News* and *Free Press* super-scribes as well as Alfred, a slippery television journalist. Jim would tell Jeff, sometimes on more than one occasion during a 162-game season; Jim would say, Jeff, my friend, keep your enemies close—and, Jeff, I refer principally to Alfred—and your bosses as far away as possible. Even after coaching, Jim estimated that Jeff detected about one-half of the total available quantity of irony contained in his partially plagiarized life dictum. But one-half was Ole Miss good and considerably greater than the absolute zero that Jim presumed of Alfred. Jim was plenty grateful for one-half.

Instead of passing through security and then turning left into an area known as the outer clubhouse—a holding pen for guests and purgatory for certain members of the press—Jim's secret entrance permitted one to slip down a short brick staircase off the parking lot to a basement door that opened with a key or a stiff credit card and shoulder. Once inside, it was a matter of knowing where to locate the light switch, because the storage room in which one found oneself was windowless and weirdly dark, as though darkness could be manufactured and made to exist there in Big Box Store quantities.

Once lit and the room safely navigated, one opened the only other door available, which led to a passageway and one additional door before then reaching a portal that opened into Jim's office. The last was thought the entrance to a closet by most because it looked that way from inside Jim's office. So elegant was everything that few would guess that behind a thick hand-carved cherry door with a gold-plated scroll adorning its masthead would lie an ugly, dreary, dank and poorly lit narrow passage leading to what felt like an abandoned UPS storage room connected by a short set of steps to the player's secured and monitored private parking area. It was inexplicable.

Jim did not know Mr. Stefanski well but what he knew meant the world to him. Mr. S. had been raised on Victorian literature and later studied 18th century physiocracy. One consequence of the former against the influence of the latter, Mr. S. had added secret passages to the Frog's already Byzantine architectural plan, the polymath lad from whom Mr. S. contracted for his addition to Giza. Mr. S. undertook to design and construct the secret passageway himself, with the help of *his boys*, which is how he referred to the junior business partners who accepted Mr. S.'s invitation to manual labor even though the sawing and nailing and painting was not their pleasure. Mr. S.'s father had been a renowned master carpenter in the old country, and so it came to pass that Mr. S.'s Business School Bedouin Blue Men apprenticed in the craft under his watchful semi-expert tutelage. Mr. S. joked that, to preserve the secret hieroglyphs they had labored so arduously to etch into its walls, he would have to have them summarily executed after the work was done, and, *Cask of Amontillado*-style, would seal their remains by candlelight and distinctive brickwork in a vault dedicated for this purpose.

***

The first thing Jim saw when he burst open his closet door was Scooter Libby in full cardiac arrest: hands pressed to chest cradling his bedside Bible, mouth agape, a shock-and-awe campaign lighting up his normally smooth pallid face. Scooter stared back at the visage of an on-coming mustached locomotive. A peep emerged as a bit of air entered or existed (Jim couldn't tell which) Scooter's overburdened lungs. Dudley Do-Right stuff, Jim thought. Life's cartoonish melodramas. *How can I help you, Nell.*

***

Lucy's mother listened attentively as they drove homeward. Dinner would be early tonight, she thought. Her daughter had an encyclopedic understanding of baseball but little sense for human beings in adult situations, including human beings who played baseball and what the sport meant for them. Lucy was bookish at heart, as was her mother, although Lucy was also fascinated by sport and in her own way was a more than capable athlete. Her mother had to concede that she certainly had never been that.

Lucy was deep into explanation for how ill-prepared The Angels looked at the plate when she added that their poor offense seemed to affect play in the field as well. On Kline's homerun, Lucy continued, she was sure that if Angels right-fielder, Mateo Lopez, would have got a good jump, taken the proper line, had practiced tracking more fly balls deep into right-field's irregular dimensions, and "D," she inserted, *had the fortitude to climb the wall like a man escaping slaughter on an island beachhead,* he might have robbed Kline of his base-rounding blow. Lopez is a cake, Lucy concluded.

Lucy's mother asked if she were rooting for The Angels, to which Lucy made a face that especially intelligent teenage girls make to their mother twenty-nine percent more often than similarly intelligent boys make to theirs and deigned not an answer before sliding in powerful Powerpuff Girls earbuds. The music could not be contained.

***

Margie had a lot on her mind, including that she wasn't sure she was over what she and Mayor Landry had discussed before the game. So much money was at stake, and she didn't want to care about money right now or ever. Everything would be okay so long as the things for which she was responsible—the things to which her late husband entrusted to her upon his sudden death, entrusted to her sole judgment—kept moving forward predictably. But Zephyr Landry, who was serving in his third consecutive term and who was *quite the talker*, Mrs. S. thought, had informed her that he was sure that the Council would not continue tax abatements which were essential for the profitable upkeep of her husband's dream. Today's opener was not a sellout. Concessions had declined three years running. The former host of baseball's all-star game was now middle-of-the-pack in league-wide fan satisfaction surveys. The last—raw, unpolished and unspun—were data strictly for league ownership but leaked somehow to the local press, adding to Margie's already steady-state business dread.

On top of this, Margie had a lump. She hadn't told anyone. She was waiting to see her family doctor, who she had known for forty years, but who was himself ailing, and, she heard only that morning, hospitalized across town at Good Samaritan. She looked forward to visiting him that very evening if she could find time after overseeing care of her now famous and even more vulnerable little prince. Dr. Sweetwater and Margie were close. When her husband passed, no one comforted her with more wisdom than Dr. Sweetwater. If he could not help her in her time of need, Margie wondered if she might see his daughter, also Dr. Sweetwater. Mary Sweetwater had once married but kept her name. She said at the wedding that there's no sweeter name nor one more quenching, the former annoyingly sappy and the last, Mrs. S. thought, ambiguous. But Mary loved her father and modelled her life on his example, and Mrs. S. could certainly appreciate that. Margie liked Mary, always had; she was only concerned that Dr. Mary was now entrusted with life, and, moreover, with death. She hoped that Sam would be on his feet. She would see him for what she thought was likely the beginning of her end.

***

It was Moisés' policy to not answer his phone or check messages prior to his post-game talk with the team, but this call was from Jack's assistant, Deborah, and one did not—certainly Moisés did not—ignore calls from Deborah or, for that matter, from the boss, the white-haired Angels General Manager Moisés called One-Eyed Jack.

Hello, Deborah, it's Moisés.

Jack's on the other line but wants to talk with you. Please hold.

Well, Deborah, I haven't talked with the team yet.

Jack will be available in a minute and he won't keep you.

Okay, sure thing, Deborah, I'll hold for you and Jack.

***

One reason that Jim was enamored of the Scooter Libby sobriquet was Walker's penchant for self-mortification in the service of dominant male authority, that is, any alpha dog who was not Jim. Scooter's Dick Cheney du jour, oddly enough, was Dave. Dave happened to be a Commodore like Scooter, but this wasn't G. Gordon Liddy stuff. Scooter wasn't eating rat or volunteering to take a bullet for his fellow Vanderbilt alumnus. Scooter would have, however, gladly served thirty months in federal table tennis instructional school for Dave. The appellation was apt albeit burdened by history.

Once Scooter had regained his meat-and-three composure, he shared that the media were still, had all this time been, waiting for Jim and The

Phenom to make their expected joint appearance, to submit to questions which they, duly badged members of the local and/or national Fourth Estate, had every right to pose. Didn't Jim understand this. Where on earth had Jim been. And where, pray tell, was the next Hal Newhouser.

***

Dave, Mrs. Stefanski, Earl, and Mayor Landry strode one by one into Jim's office. Where's Konrad Lorenz, Jim thought. Jim's office was a large space: four additional were easily accommodated. But when Sammy entered wearing protective gear, and then Jeff, an American cigarette glued to his lower lip, Jim thought it was getting stuffy.

Look, everyone. The kid told me that he had to bug-out, okay. He told me....

I do not understand, Jimmy. The people are going to want to hear from that boy.

Mayor, look, he's not a politician, he's an eighteen-year-old boy....

Jim, my word. You're the manager. You know that I am that boy's guardian.

I know, Mrs. Stefanski. Jeff and I are going to look after him, I promise.

Well, I should think so. But we must consider our customers as well. I think you ought to pay more attention to the bottom line, Jim. Why aren't you talking with the media. Come to think of it, why aren't you in that press room right this minute.

What my sister means, Jim, is that it's getting hot in there. Walker called and he's in a lather. And I'm not talking about the temperature, you know that, right.

Jim, why are you not in that press room.

I think the press had most of their questions answered. I gave them background. I hit on Kline's offseason regime, which I could see they simply ate up. If the kid's vamoose, as Jim says he is, then maybe we should shut it down. Call it a day.

Have you lost what few marbles you got, Mr. Dave. This is not something about which you go mum and turn out the lights. My sister is right about customers. They won't take kindly to a news blackout. Imagine the push-back, for gosh sake. The press is…you know, they're going to smell blood in the water and none of us wants that.

As someone who's campaigned in every neighborhood in this city, some of them with police escort, the people need uplift of the sort this young star has given them.

Look, all due respect, but Uplift has gone and shot out the back door. He told me he had to leave, that he couldn't stay for this commotion, and who can blame him. Hell, the more I stay here, the more I wish I'd had gone with him, tell you the honest truth.

Jim's right. Let's say we've said enough. I think my statements were enough.

David, please. I am surprised at you. You must look at this not from a people perspective but from a business perspective. We're losing money. We're standing here and losing money.

Can I say something. Can I…. Me and Jim have been together a long time, as you all know. We know baseball. We know ballplayers. This kid's clearly not ready for that scrum. He's barely ready to be here at all. In fact….

Jeff, thanks, but let's take note of a few things. Mrs. S., your little prince has been gone for probably ten or fifteen minutes, maybe longer, I don't know. Anyway, he's not coming back. Dave talked to the press, so we're covered there. If I go in there, there'll be all kinds of questions about pitch selection, about those twists and turns we saw on the mound—Sammy is going to get those questions too, aren't you Sammy— and I don't see how any of this helps. The more we talk, the more other teams are going to listen. Saramachi will be watching the video, you can be sure of that. More talk, more distraction. And, it's evident, we've got a fella who's not so keen on the spotlight.

Skip is right. He was incredible on the mound, but the kid and I barely talked.

I think maybe you should send Jeff out if you don't want to go, Jim. Have Jeff answer some of these questions.

If Jim ain't going, I'm not going.

Enough. Enough of this. I am the team principal owner and I will decide what to do. Sammy, could you please step out.

Mrs. Stefanski, with all due respect....

Gentleman, I have decided that our manager, Jim Murry, will go into that press briefing room and answer questions.

But Mrs. S....

Jim, the gentlewoman who pays your salary has made up her mind. I will go after you-know-who. I'm the one who doesn't need to be here.

***

Driving with baseball cleats is not recommended. It's probably illegal for good reason. This is especially relevant when merging onto a highway, even more so when the situation in question is a narrow entrance into a sharp turn typical of older city exchanges where the geography of the urban core far preceded the development of the highway system, which subsequently had to wrap itself around any number of floating ribs, gangly appendages, and severed extremities. Even the advent of automatic cars, driver services, and the light rail explosion, hadn't significantly reduced traffic congestion nor meaningfully enhanced highway safety. Cleated, somewhat inexperienced, teary-eyed distracted drivers only made things much, much worse.

The eighteen-wheeler that bore down on the Toyota had itself less than 5,000 miles on its odometer. It was hauling empty containers, which reduced its weight and thus its momentum. Its long-haul driver was fresh and wide awake. While traffic volume was rising, it hadn't yet reached its rush-hour peak. These weighed on the one side.

The eighteen-wheeler was exceeding a safe speed through the turn. The driver had seen it coming but nonetheless allowed a sport utility vehicle to box his truck into the slow lane on a two-lane mid-town turn. The visibility on the turn was limited. Cars merging from the entrance ramp materialized, because of the grades, curves, and angles involved, at the last second even for drivers benefitting from a crow's nest.

The Toyota pilot and part-time baseball bombardier zipped along, *The Black Keys* his pacemaker. He checked his side mirror and he noted first that it was filled with a sizable fast-moving truck and, second, that he was quickly running out of on-ramp. Rather than strike the barrier ahead, the driver of the late-model Camry slammed down on his brakes, or so attempted. Because he was wearing baseball cleats rather than smooth-soled shoes, his feet slipped off the side of the pedal. He had slammed so hard, so violently against the old, worn, slippery brake pedal, that both of his feet fell asunder.

The car slid and heaved. Captain Cold Sweat reapplied the brakes. The truck's horn caused all the world to look over its shoulder to see what was about to happen. The sport utility sped-up and swerved in dialogue with anticipated and, regardless, easily recognizable evasive action. The Toyota came to a stop inches from the starboard guardrail and less than one foot from a thick sand bar at the bow. Hamburger and fry refuse came ashore as a Level 5 tsunami and nestled over the whole of the forward interior, including dashboard air-conditioning vents, where it would stay forever.

Reggie Ross saw the brake lights ahead and slowed.

Grandpa, I think there may have been an accident.

I don't see no fire.

Grandpa, I'm serious.

I see it now. That's a dangerous ramp, always has been.

Let's help that man.

Reggie, he don't need our help. Everyone's got phones nowadays.

He might be hurt.

He ain't hurt. Just scared, probably.

I'm pulling over.

Reggie, you got a big heart, son.

***

When Jack's voice finally found Moisés' ears, it was without proper introduction. Deborah put him straight though. She didn't say: Jack's ready now. Are you ready.

Jack says the team looked wildly ill-prepared. He asks why Moisés didn't bunt and why he didn't use more pinch batters. He asks why Moisés didn't at least get thrown out for protesting Nuzzi's criminal strike zone. Was Moisés resting on laurels. What laurels does Moisés think he possesses upon which he might rest, asked Jack.

***

Lucy's father worked from home and so was there when she and her mother pulled into the drive. He beamed when others talked of Lucy. He might share that she beat out over two-hundred applicants for the position with the team. He surprised himself and Lucy both by so appreciating her spunky fouled ball girl thing. (Her dad was one of her first followers.) Having kept an eye on the game and even some of the post-game coverage, he was aware that the post-game press conference had been delayed but would soon commence. His wheelchair, oxygen, and other *equipment*, as he called his life-sustaining devices, kept him home, while Lucy's mother's job kept her away, but here they were all together, and instead of mom and dad being at the game, as would be normal and expected on opening day, they could at least watch some of the aftermath together. It was some game, Dan knew. In fact, although he wasn't a baseball guy, Dan Higgins was pretty sure that there had never been a game quite like it. He pondered the meaning the word *unique*, which he knew was dangerous to ever use.

***

Sammy thought about the press conference. He wasn't sure he understood why he wasn't talking with the press. Some had come to his locker for a quote and he had done his best to offer them. One local station, a friend of his, asked him for a stand-up.

Sammy Robertson, you just caught a perfect game, how do you feel.

Sammy, The Angels whiffed all day long. How did you feel.

Sammy, did you call that knuckleball. How did you feel.

***

Mrs. S. was satisfied with her performance and relieved to start making calls. She left voicemail and sent text messages. Her network was activated, as it was routinely. She acted in a mechanical manner that belied the dread which she knew to accompany such times, such unknowns. Dread may be depression's kissing cousin, she thought. Except for losing Mr. S., and what her Little Prince bestowed upon her as a matter of course, and maybe a few other things, Mrs. S. hadn't any experience of dread.

***

No, I'm okay. Really, I'm fine.

Hey, you're that pitcher, aren't you.

No, I'm fine. I'm going to back up.

Sure, we'll back up too. It may help, the two cars.

I understand. Thank you for stopping. I appreciate it.

Me and my Gramps wanted to be sure you were okay.

I am. Thank you. Thank you very much, you and your grandfather.

You're more than welcome, friend.

That means a lot. It does. You're both so kind but I should be on my way.

***

The Angels locker room was businesslike. There was shared recognition that opening day did not go well. There was also, however, shared recognition that the kid was unhittable. Never had the words nasty, dirty, and wicked been used in so concentrated of a time/space as in Mr. S.'s visitor's locker room after this opening day game. Shoulders shrugged. Weederman, The Angels' starter, required no consolation.

Craig, tough out there today.

It was a quality start.

Yeah, but to give up two runs and never be in it like that.

It's all about giving my team a chance to win. I did my job. That's baseball.

How do you feel.

My arm feels great.

***

Sagacious Sage took some pressure off his back, which had been bent since the weekend's brush with lawn work. Perspicacious Wordsmith nearly missed the seat at which he aimed his ample behind. It may have been that his blood sugar was tanking. No one wanted to miss what Jim would say to the assembled throng. They knew the kid was not coming. Paul Revere had raced ahead, sowing upset left and right. But Walker's Late Afternoon Ride did not fluster the most semi-erudite. Sage and Wordsmith could envision Jim's office and an in-depth interview on a near horizon. They would take turns getting at what was meaningful. They would develop themes, and, indirectly, interrogate burning social issues. You toss fifty or more types of pitches between sixty and two-hundred miles per hour, which is great, but tell us about your upbringing, when you first knew that you were destined for greatness, any siblings with intellectual delays, mobility challenges, emergent mental illnesses; of these, how many.

***

Dr. Sweetwater awoke from a nap and felt well enough to flick on the television. He liked baseball even before he met the Stefanskis. Since he was nearly a family friend, he felt an obligation, as well as a mild desire, to tune in. Margie would get around to asking if he had seen the game or was following the team. He was late to the action but maybe he could still catch the tail-end or at least he could learn what had transpired.

***

Lucy, mom, and dad gathered around a computer screen that was their television. The used three different kinds of chairs. Chez Higgins had a dozen more just like them, all unique.

***

Sammy, who was among the final one-third of players hanging around the clubhouse, grabbed a seat so he could watch the press conference in comfort. The players' leather chairs were oversized and overstuffed. Footstools were loveseats.

***

Jim was preceded into the press room by Earl, who was compelled to lead the procession. Mayor Landry was next and went directly to the front of the not-large, wide more than deep, room. He sat near the open center aisle that was maintained so that cameras positioned in the rear had a clear shot of the podium. Jim and Jeff paused to kibitz with back-benchers. Scooter danced the pee-pee dance, which, as he did this so often it had to be purposeful, reminded Jim of Squealer from *Animal Farm*. Jeff stopped before the platform, seeming to salute as Jim passed onto and toward the microphone-laden podium. When the camera lights powered up, Jim realized that he wasn't wearing his ball cap. He would have taken it off regardless, he reasoned. He despised hats.

First question, Jim. Was history made today.

Yes.

Well, following up, can you say more about that. What sort of history was made.

Whenever something happens, history is made. We're making history right now. What just happened, happened. You can't change it. What's more, it will affect what comes next. And so on.

Jim, right. I see where you're going. What I'm asking, Was *baseball* history made today. Did we see something we've never seen before.

It's interesting that you put it that way. So, you're saying that which is history is that which *hasn't* before happened, something—if I follow you—that *doesn't* come from what came before it.

I'm not trying to get philosophical, Jim. Honestly, I am simply asking for your thoughts on today's incredible game.

I thought we played well and I'm glad we won. It's a team sport, friends. What you saw was our team scoring a few runs more than their team. We won the game, made few if any mistakes, and I don't think we had any injuries to speak of. I'm satisfied.

Yes, but Jim, seriously, your...what is he...eighteen-year-old opening day starting pitcher just pitched a perfect game. A perfect game, Jim. And he made it look easy. His first game was a perfect game. It's your first perfect game, too. I don't get it.

Look, I'm answering your questions. Give me some question marks.

Let me try. Jim, why isn't he here to answer questions himself.

Well, it's both simple and complicated. For one, we've got a policy for young players like that, which limits the amount of press exposure. I sent him home.

A policy.

Yep, we want to protect players from too much distraction. We have a team of veterans. You can talk with them or me or Jeff or whomever you want. You've got Walker, too. That's his job is to talk with you guys

You're being unreasonable.

Am I. Maybe you are. Have you thought about that. Have you.

Jim, please, we're only doing our jobs.

So am I, gentlemen and gentlewomen, so am I.

***

Dave wasn't sure where all the bellicosity was coming from. He stood at the door hoping to catch Jim's eyes, but with little hope of so doing because the camera lights made that impossible. His statements had gone well, and now this combative tone. He had been asked about the knuckleball, to which he replied that knuckleballs were not uncommon, not unfair, not in any way a prohibited pitch, and that, obviously, the kid's knuckleball was pretty good. He had been asked if the kid was mocking or paying homage to Luis Tiant, Jim Palmer, Dan Quisenberry, Scott McGregor, and other pitchers. He had said that he wasn't sure that the kid had those individuals in mind at all, but if he had, that imitation was the highest form of flattery. He had been asked about how the team had signed the kid. Where was he from. What was his prior baseball experience. Dave had replied, truthfully, that he did not know much about the young man other than he seemed a good enough sort of fellow. Mrs. S. had introduced him to her general manager and manger, Dave shared, and Mrs. S. had proposed his initial contract, which was modest, and, under the circumstances, quite rightly so. It was all straightforward, Dave assured. Once Jim and Jeff had got a look at him, they accepted Mrs. S.'s suggestion that he might make a good opening day pitcher. Apparently, based on Mrs. S.'s telling, Mr. Stefanski had always wanted to have a surprise opening day pitcher, but the opportunity eluded him. Dave felt good about his performance. It wasn't as though he had declared himself the second coming of Christ.

***

Pulling up to his apartment did not entail significant public exposure, whereas leaving the car, however, might. Off comes the damned cleats. Off comes the uniform top. In races the hero of today's opening tilt with Angels. Time for some much-needed rest, some much needed sleep. Off comes the lid on his bedside nightstand. *Down goes Fraizer.*

***

Hud was not like the others. He tuned into the news conference because he had a genuine interest in the game: its history, its nuances, its subtleties. He sat on the Angels' bus and with earbuds in he watched Jim hold-forth, his eyes in his lap. Will had been wiped off the face of the earth by the most dominant pitcher to ever throw a game. To hear Seth Franken and Hector Gonzalez talk, what had happened was historically unprecedented, which Hud thought perhaps redundant. Hud could hear the concern welling in Jim's voice. He felt the tension mounting between Jim and mediated world.

***

Jim, let's put it this way: were you surprised that Angels batters were unable to even foul-off a pitch. Not one all day.

Ah, they may have fouled a few. It's hard to tell. Robertson was all over that stuff.

We've looked at it, Jim. There were no foul-tips. Does that surprise you.

Yes.

Well, why.

It's unusual.

It's not unusual, Jim, it's unprecedented.

If you say so.

Well, you *know* so, Jim.

Look, I like the history of the game as much as y'all, but I do not, as you say, know so. I've not had time to research it. Have you.

It stands to reason, Jim.

Jim, I have a question.

Go ahead, then.

Did you call for a knuckleball in the ninth inning. Did you call for a knuckleball to Will Huddlescamp.

What about the submarine. What about that one.

Well, I don't.... Jeff, did we call for a knuckleball there at the end. I can't recall.

Ah, Jim, you know…

Speak up, we can't hear you.

Well, there was so much going on right then. We had Sanchez…. We were thinking about who we might bring in if we needed to.

Bring in Sanchez. What are you guys talking about.

Jim, it's a straightforward question. Are you saying you do or do not recall if you called for a knuckleball. A knuckleball, Jim.

Hey, now. Jim's job is darn complex….

Our microphones can't hear you if you don't get closer or talk louder.

Well, you know. I was saying that there's a lot going on at the end of a game like that.

Listen, I probably signaled something to Sammy, and he signaled something to the mound, and who knows what scrambled eggs came of it, okay. It doesn't matter.

Jim, did you or didn't you. Or are you saying a rank rookie who's never pitched in a professional baseball game before today took it upon himself to show up Will Huddlescamp with a knuckleball.

Nobody showed anyone up.

Are you going to answer the question posed to you.

I already have and as far as Jim Murry is concerned, this press conference is *over*. Scooter can answer the rest of your damn questions.

***

Hud ignored the phone rumbling in his pocket. Lucy sat pensive on a stool writing a poem in her head that she would later post as Fouled Ball Girl. Mr. Ross was relieved to be home and grateful for an opening day victory, grateful for the ride, grateful for his grandson, grateful for his encounter with a real-live ballplayer, an honest-to-god human being, who turned out to be a person like he was, alone, yes sir, and maybe a bit lost.

***

Never churlish a day in her life, Dr. Mary Sweetwater stepped into her father's suite to find him head in hand with a sickened look on his face. What is it, daddy. Daddy said that the Earth was rotating and orbiting much too fast. Mary glanced out a window.

***

Moisés held his head in hands, which was not like him nor the way a manager should act after a loss. He sat behind the lead motor coach driver and kept bowed nearly the entire way to the team hotel. The driver signaled. After traffic cleared, the coach swung wide around and under the expansive hotel overhang designed to protect a hundred motorists at a time against the elements. Today, the massive sheltered area and the decorative fountain that it curved about provided welcome shade and noticeably cooler temperatures, not to mention the rushing sound of lapping water, all of which helped Moisés calm himself after what had been an especially stressful day at work.

FIVE

The Little Prince settled in preparation for sleep. He put aside what others wanted from him to focus on that which he wanted for himself. He presumed that he was no longer Mrs. S.'s secret Phenom, but he avoided thinking about himself as a figure burst onto sports radio and television talk shows across the Baseball Nation. He flirted with self-protection in this way. That's probably how he had survived this long.

The Little Prince resolved to take advantage of the golden opportunity before him and continue work on his long-term project, his masterwork, his measured response to Steinbeck. He admired Steinbeck's Baja philosophy and his field journalism. He had carefully studied his and Charlie's cross-country exploration of aging and masculinity. (The southern racism was particularly unforgettable, but The Little Prince didn't like that Steinbeck had forever colored his appreciation for poodles.) There was the marine biology and Steinbeck's case for basic social democracy. The Little Prince had acquainted himself with these and more through past Steinbeck immersions.

The Little Prince admired many aspects of Steinbeck, but there was no way he was going to absolve George for what he did to Lenny. The Little Prince fixated on this point. George was armed. He might have threatened, and, if need be, laid siege to Lenny's pursuers. George was intelligent. He might have offered a soliloquy on man's inhumanity to man, enlisting Lenny as quixotic combatant. Why didn't George point the gun to his own head, and, if need be, given the mob a lesson in self-sacrifice, in responsibility. Mightn't that have incited their pause and iced their raging heads.

Instead, as the Little Prince knew all too well, George put a bullet in the back of his friend's head. George bent to the mob's fury and was rewarded by being stitched back into a now-worthless social fabric. The Little Prince was haunted by Lenny's mercy-killing, so called. Steinbeck's dog should have eaten the final manuscript just as it had the original. The Little Prince fell asleep dreaming of dog shit.

***

The morning lit his disheveled apartment. The Little Prince was ready to make himself coffee when he noticed *The Pearl* laying on a sticker-covered guitar case. His mind was a-jumble. Coffee and blood sloshed together by time the Little Prince imagined an author roaming Vietnam, extolling the virtue of Armageddon. If John Wayne Gacy Steinbeck entertained men and boys with tales of mercy-killings, providing them distraction, perhaps the engaged artist would help save his son and other father's sons from Keats- and Shelley-like premature finalities. Maybe, thought the Little Prince, this explained Steinbeck's bizarre behavior.

The Little Prince wasn't convinced of his analysis. Maybe Steinbeck was an aging artist who just couldn't square himself with something as *sissy* as giving peace a chance. Maybe he was triggered at the thought of losing a war, which, in his mind, was tantamount to collective impotence. In any event, one thing was clear: Steinbeck had set about to sell Vietnam the way exalted artistic integrity would later sell motor scooters, vodka, and John Varvatos. Not exactly Vera, Chuck and Dave, but, the Little Prince supposed, surviving what they survived, these artists might as well make a buck. Utterly disappointing, but so it goes.

The Little Prince then put a tablespoon of Michigan's Thumb and a pony of Wisconsin's Teat in his coffee. He drank what his late grandmother, a Catholic school wiseacre circa 1942, called cough syrup. I drink coffee, she would say, you drink cough syrup. The Little Prince reflected on what he suspected was the mildest rebuke ever leveled while sipping the weakest bean ever brewed. Only hours into his debut, unbeknownst to him, as a Fab Four famous professional baseball player, the Little Prince's habits were anything but healthy, his circumstances borderline alarming. Sanchez drove a candy apple Tesla to his très lux spread up Far Hills Drive; yesterday's starting pitcher, supported by a sinecure designed to not spoil him, lived apart from his regiment and bourgeois standards of home and hearth, a candied Braeburn floating in the toilet in his cherished domicile's one of two federally designated superfund sites.

It was 10:30 a.m. and his phone's mailbox had reached maximum capacity hours ago. There was no point spending the rest of the day responding to a melting Greenland glacier of messages, all of them urgent. He sat wearing his uniform trousers from the afternoon before, fastened with thick black belt and large black buckle. Full of cough syrup and whatever else, the unexpected hard knock at his door sent him into shock. The Youth was in no condition to receive company. He never was, and never would be.

A siren entered as familiar aria above the 4/4 meter of doorway clamoring. It was Mrs. S., as he knew it must be. Her agents had spied his Toyota the night before and it was decided in conference to let the boy sleep, his soul, Mrs. S. prayed, to keep. But it was now mid-morning and time had come for wiping slumber. Mrs. S. appeared as an irrepressible agent of daylight who insisted that the Little Prince rise and shine and carry weight. His guardian was a driver of bondsmen. She had spent a lifetime taking no no's for answers and no prisoners, too. Except this one. The Little Prince was her exception.

Ahh…. I'm not dressed.

Well, pull something on, dear. I need to talk with you.

Can we talk later. I'm not awake yet.

We shall get something to eat. Get dressed, please.

Can you come back in a few hours.

I could but I am a busy person and there is much to do.

How about one hour.

Alright. Thirty minutes. Be ready.

He listened from behind the windowless door but didn't hear a vehicle pull away. Mrs. S. was planning to wait for him, working from her car, impatiently consulting her diamond-encrusted bracelet. He knew her better than she knew him, he thought. He had met Mrs. S. years prior at the Boys & Girls Club. Their relationship hadn't really become serious, though, until his confinement at The Villages, an exclusive semi-rural residential shelter for youth dangerous to themselves and others and for whom 24/7 care was court-ordered. If one hadn't cut themselves and probably resisted medical dispensation—and if one hadn't more than once demonstrated capacity to sever the community's fragile and exposed limbs—then chances were that a bloke wasn't ready to pay their dues at the bandaged Mar-a-Lago.

The Villages had been the turning point. What had begun as fan fiction had turned into Dostoevsky wrapped in a riddle. Mrs. S.'s adorable baby alligator seemed to be growing into a rough-skinned man-eating reptile with a yawning cavity full of teeth and appetite for sublime adventure. Who knew what he was anymore. He felt blurry. The Little Prince even said of himself that it was probably too late to flush him down the toilet.

***

Not long into his incarceration, the Little Prince realized that his fellow villagers were scarred without exception. They had multiple diagnoses and recent attempts about which they were expected to endlessly share.

SAY HEY LITTLE PRINCE

The most artfully incorrigible dodger of them all believed few of his fellow *boys*, as he playfully called them, were on good terms with the taken for granted. Few could define intellect, he thought, let alone engage one. (Some could, certainly, but they had been purposively distributed among the houses and groups, and, in any case, rarely enjoyed opportunity to compare notes.) Most Villagers hadn't read anything of consequence, including their permanent records. When he was not cooking for his housemates, making use of skills won on a lark at two short-order universities, the Little Prince recorded his compadres' life-stories on four-track tapes he kept rolling in his high school garage band memory. He played some ball, too. Fellow villagers provided wide berth. To many of them, the Little Prince was from another world. He never argued their point.

Lost in a wooded retreat, The Youth gazed up at myriad mounted riders who ministered to one another more than to him, and for whom he and his type might as well have been non-existent except for the profit in them. He was amused by their definition of authority, which he understood, not inaccurately, as power accepted as legitimate by those over whom power is exercised. On one of their weekends together, Mrs. S. heard him out on the subject, about which he was passionate, and in reply she explained that stopping at a stoplight was submitting to authority and wasn't it a good idea that we heeded stoplights. The Little Prince belied his years in this and in other respects, for Mrs. S.'s dissertation on mutually assured reciprocity was, he said firmly, premised on blatant falsehoods. His parents were gone, and, besides Mrs. S., he was forsaken. One thing after another since set in him a near-congenital conviction that a few can run stoplights whenever and wherever they please, while others—so many others, a planet full of others—patiently waste away at desert crossroads waiting for, of all things, a sign.

***

The master of the Millsaps Residence of Strawberry Hill would have signed onto to this point of view, if he had a chance to understand it. Jeff was the eighth highest paid pitching coach in baseball outside of Japan, and he never had much good to say about authority. Growing up in Jeff's Mississippi was like struggling for fresh air in the bottom of a spittoon. Every elected official, it felt to him—every minister, school principal, bank president, newspaper editor, police chief, car salesperson, and Junior League charity ball chair—were as corrupt and self-serving as they come. Their mendacity was literary.

The University of Mississippi hadn't provided the respite Jeff anticipated when he arrived to begin his stint as a scholar-athlete. During his five years in Oxford—the best and worst of times, he told people—six cheating scandals rocked Rebel Athletics. Ole Miss escaped meaningful sanction only by a bent whisker on the infraction committee's chinny-chin-chin. Yet, as Jeff and perhaps few others suspected, these were minor violations in comparison to the purloined letter fraud that lay at the heart of the institution, where barely passable earned a B and anything legible earned an A. Jeff loved baseball but truly abhorred mendacity. For Jeff, Oxford was an Ole Miss B.

Millsaps was smarter than he sounded and looked. He would have delighted in the opportunity to loll about the bullpen and batting cage with his new and evidently brainy pitcher, his William Faulkner in Hollywood, his junior General Abner Doubleday.

Jeff positioned himself in front of a widescreen television to watch highlights and commentary about yesterday's home opener. He wouldn't depart for the stadium for another hour and this was a good time to review the local, national, and worldwide reaction to yesterday's epochal performance. Franz Klammer *squared*, said Austrian TV, referencing Austria's most famous downhill skiing gold medalist. Jeff was pleased with himself for watching Austrian TV and for not batting an eye at the reference. As breathtaking as *Free Solo*, said the Lifetime channel, which caused Jeff to frown and pick up his phone. Jeff also flipped though the local newspapers' respective morning editions. What surprised him was the balance in the reporting, where equal weight was given to the Angels' staggering ineptitude as was devoted to his boy's pitching virtuosity. Weederman, apparently, was wild and undisciplined, whereas his guy was a nine-foot tall basketball player. Jeff watched as Luis Tiant, Tim Wakefield, and The Quiz voted Huddlescamp off the planet. Jeff's head was on a free-form swivel. The more he watched, the more he realized that he had not processed recent events.

There's a lot we do not know about baseball's newest Phenom, but the radar gun, friends, does not lie. The gun does not lie.

His homage to The Greats was splendid entertainment. He's bringing fun back to the game. Some Angel should have brought a table leg to the plate.

What if he does this every game. What would be the point. As the league did when it permitted batters to be automatically walked, they should issue a win when it's this kid's turn in the rotation. Why throw four intentional balls. Give him the win.

His arm won't last the season. I know he threw only eighty-one pitches, but with that kind of velocity and those sort of angles and breaks, I don't see him pitching in the second half. Look at what happened to Wood. We've seen this movie.

What I found disturbing, frankly, was the humiliation involved. Would you cheer NBA Champions as they slam-dunk on 5th graders. I feel dirty. That wasn't fun.

The Angels deserve relegation, mate. Down to the minors. Moisés Saramachi's days are numbered. His team quit on him, apparently during spring training.

I appreciate perfection as much as the next person, but the whole point of sport is competition and yesterday's game was anything but a competition.

Let me push back on that. Competition isn't the essence of sport. Sport is about performance within proscribed limits. He was brilliant. I think we saw sport at its finest.

If you're right, no one is going to pay to watch sport at its finest. They'll look for something without a preordained conclusion. That's where the excitement comes in. With this kid, it's over when it's over, and it's over when he steps on the mound.

You're missing the beauty. His pitches weren't pitches; they were aesthetic ideas.

This isn't about art. Let me make this abundantly clear: Jim Murry's surprise opening day starting pitcher is a vital threat to baseball as an entertainment industry.

***

Mrs. S. returned ahead of schedule, but the Little Prince was ready to take advantage of his second chance. He may have forgotten underarm deodorant, while a quick lick of his teeth suggested that he may have forgotten to brush as well. But his wet hair and evidently liberal use of South Sea Bubble Body Wash would provide Mrs. S. assurance that her starving would-be dining companion would be seated at Étienne's Bistro on Wyandot, which he knew was her preferred mid-morning brunch restaurant.

Given Mrs. S.'s business, it was not surprising to find her behind the wheel of one of her brands' most luxurious, fully loaded models. Noting that its manufacturer was American was like observing wheels and tires, so much as national identity meant anything under the hood in the long-integrated and interdependent global automobile industry. Thirty-seven semi-independent countries had colluded in creation of Mrs. S.'s international space station, but only one, General Motors Corp., had the wanton temerity to engrave its fleur-de-lis on her bonnet, bumper, and black leather dash.

He asked himself why someone as wealthy and as old as Mrs. Stefanski would eschew a professional driver. He suspected that chauffeurs, like all service staff, were destined to be royal pains in the derrière. Mrs. S wouldn't be able to go anywhere without a tail wagging the dog. Nor could she talk without some Big Ears Johnson eavesdropping on her conversation. He thought of the public relations debacle that might ensue if Mrs. S. showed up at the stadium or, for that matter, at a place like The Villages, impersonating Cruella de Ville. Not good for sales. Not good for contract negotiations. Not good for lost boys salivating for Étienne's pig meat and conch special.

***

So, listen to me for a moment.

I'm listening.

Oh, dear. How much aftershave did you use, sweetie.

Ah, it's my body wash. I think I forgot to shave.

Well, listen. You are an exceptional athlete. What you did yesterday has everyone talking. I mean, everyone, dear. You have great potential and I don't want you to squander it, do you see.

Yeah.

I want you to contribute, to leave your mark.

I don't want to leave a mark.

Écoute, mon cher. Mr. Stefanski and I, as you know, had no children of our own. If he were here, I know he would want me to support you in this mission of yours.

I don't understand.

Your mission, dear, to play baseball. Or so I guess it must be. To set the world on fire as a baseball player. And what a start you've made.

That's not my mission.

***

The word *mission* released the Little Prince from his moorings at *Etienne's* and sent him floating. How many beasts had tested whether their mammal superiors were ready for capsule time, had given the best days of their lives, so that their masters and commanders could conquer the final frontier. To the Little Prince, mission meant military and military meant death. Little space kittens, he knew, survived reentry only to meet Lt. Colonel Vivisection; space monkeys gave their evolved cerebral cortices so that men, overwhelmingly, could rest assured. Mission impossible, thought the Little Prince. He even mumbled it audibly.

The Little Prince reminisced about Dayton, Ohio, his place of birth. He began life as a capuchin and the hospital where he was delivered was soon converted to rent-controlled apartments. Daytonians of all primate varieties were raised to venerate Orville Wright, Wilbur Wright, and Neil Armstrong, the trinity who established the southwestern Ohio market as ground zero for saleable aviation pioneer history.

The Little Prince was an energetic simian who spent his nubile days swinging through the suspended aerial killing machines at the U.S. Air Force Museum, attracted by acres of war matériel, and, he was perhaps too young to appreciate, everyday free admission. The museum's Presidential Air Force One Collection resided in the military-industrial complex and an onsite IMAX theater, which charged a premium, featured whatever the IMAX film circuit made available without regard to thematic consistency. Polar bears. Power Grids. The museum IMAX would screen anything.

In the Little Prince's youth, and before most of its businesses closed, Dayton's skies were regularly filled with soft diplomacy air shows and ambient celebration of gravity-defying ingenuity, including blimps. A

Daytonian could hardly avoid tripping over Flyers, brother reenactors, and Huffman's Field poets trolling in hope of turning rocky Midwestern soil into windswept North Carolina beaches. The fact that Henry Ford had long ago absconded to Michigan with the authentic Wright Bicycle Shop went officially unacknowledged. In Dayton, Ford's Greenfield Village was nothing but a poisoned brownfield in need of reclamation.

Unexpectedly, the U.S. Air Force Museum IMAX screened a film about helicopters, but the Little Prince, a sound- and life-sensitive boy, ran crying from the noise after only a few minutes. He did the same when an F-15 Eagle, its flaps fully extended, scrapped frothy foam off hospitality tent tops at the local air show. The Little Prince could not stand what others took for granted as noise. It was like to kill him.

Ear-infections and ear-tubes, immigration to Tennessee and then to Upstate New York, youth football and diagnosed ADHD, preceded early onset cutting, eating disorders, drug abuse, and five attempted suicides. How quickly the genus homo who hugs with arms and legs grows into an adolescent with a mind of his own. How rapidly a battered and abused child grows into a teen with operational knowledge of pain biochemistry. Around this time, the Little Prince surmised that self and knowledge were combustible double-edged words. Around this time, his kinship with Brother Vonnegut flowered, and, as homage, he named his new dog Kurt. Not unexpectedly, The Little Prince wasn't mature enough to care for Kurt.

***

Dr. Sweetwater stared at his Good Samaritan breakfast of steamed Zanzibar River Worm with sides of Moroccan Camel Mucus and Palauan Bat Guano. He'd seen his share of nasty hospital bento boxes, but this took the cake. Nutritionists, not lawyers, should be the first against the wall, or so he mused. Sam conceded that his lack of appetite hadn't much to do with the tray of grubs. He pushed it away in favor of hot tea.

Sam didn't mind that Margie had cancelled the night previous. He was only bothered that she didn't herself call, that she had her nephew intercede. The good doctor, Samuel C. Sweetwater of the University of Michigan Medical School and board-certified for over forty years, suffered fools either not at all or only because he couldn't find an easy workaround. He was near to understanding that the root cause of his upset had nothing to do with court jester, Dandy Vandy Walker Evans Stefanski, when, in that moment, Sam turned his attitude, as he had learned to do early in life, and became in an instant satisfied that Margie had promised to visit later that morning. He needed to get cleaned up. He guessed that he must look like a greenish-gray worm wiggling in the Salween's rich silt. It made him think of a new line of work: Imported Sweetwater's Salween Silt. *It will grow anything, even the dreams of your lost relatives.* His lips turned up, then down. He wasn't sure that he wanted to doctor any longer or enjoy baseball.

***

Jeff's SUV had a hands-free phone system that allowed passengers to converse with an unlimited number of callers, whose voices were syncopated via a baker's dozen high-fidelity speakers positioned for listening pleasure throughout the roomy cabin. Two speakers were under the back seats. It was G.M.'s latest novelty. It was called Mozart®.

Jeff, are you coming.

Yeah, Jim, I'm coming. I'll be there in twenty.

Wait, Dave is calling too.

Don't answer that, Jeff. I god bless 'ed beseech you.

Dave, it's Jeff. Jim's on the line, too.

Good morning, men. We must discuss…

I know, don't tell me: Akihiko's tweet.

No, what. He tweeted. What did he tweet.

Nothing. Forget about it. It was partly in Japanese.

We need to discuss the kid's next start.

Dave, Sato is today's pitcher. Let's take it one day at a time, shall we.

Yeah, Dave, I have to agree there. Let's recall that we have thirteen pitchers on this roster, not one.

Jeff, where are you, anyhow.

Well, I'm turning onto Wabash.

You're not in the clubhouse. Jim, are you in the clubhouse.

You know I am, Dave. We saw each other thirty minutes ago.

Let's meet in Jim's office at noon. We can have lunch brought in.

Wait, Sammy is calling.

Jeff, damn it.

Hi, Sammy. Dave and Jim are on the line too.

Oh, hey gentlemen. Good morning. I was calling Jeff to talk about the kid's next start. And did you see what Sato put out there. Whoa.

***

Jim used to think managing was principally baseball related. He thought he was qualified to manage because he knew the rules of the game as well as any umpire or league official, and he knew technique, strategy, and could draw from a wealth of situational experience whenever he needed to make an in-game decision. While others cast shade, he also knew talent when he saw it, not from years of scouting, but from a seemingly innate appreciation for excellence borne of his own theoretically informed playing experience. He was, and had always been, a student of the game. He could listen to a bat rip the air or a ball striking a glove and know more than most about whether a fresh prospect had a chance to ever see light by Double A. Jim was the genuine article. But, as it turned out, knowledge of this type had little to do with his job.

Managing was first and foremost about people and people's emotions. It was secondly about communication about and with people and their emotions. Baseball itself was a distant third. Thankfully, humans were easy for Jim. Inspired by Mr. Stefanski, Jim had read extensively in several genres and would no less sit with a statistician than commit a social science. He was the calculated antithesis of *Moneyball*.

Communication was more difficult. Jim was accused of being circumspect with some, unwilling to lavish praise on others. In some quarters, he was accused of failing to share information up and down the organizational hierarchy, in effect, denying his colleagues the benefit of his, they would say, admired thinking. Chewing on an Oval and holding forth with reporters were easily within his repertoire. No one questioned Jim's baseball bona fides. But when it came to assessing with any degree of certitude that his players knew what he thought of them or that his coaches understood their roles or that his ownership was confident in his business savvy, then on these and similar points of interpersonal communication, Jim knew that he could use some work. It was unlikely that the world would come around to him. He thought of such things after hanging up.

***

Mrs. S. was not pleased or inspired in any way to watch a paper napkin be used to wipe drips from still-wet hair, moisture that was accumulating on his obviously still-damp face and neck. She was also curious why her preferred brunch establishment had offered paper napkins in the first place. She decided then and there to deliver this man-child into Jim's able custody as soon as the professional athlete with whom she dined finished his stack of specially ordered chocolate pancakes, the lower levels of which were bathing in a Keystone Pipeline spill of warmed syrup and butter. Mrs. S. had a doctor to see and a pit in her stomach the size of the lump in her neck. The oozing crêpe de chocolate hadn't helped, but the on-going napkin fiasco put her over the edge.

***

Walker, having reflected on Jim's slip of the tongue at the press conference, was busily devising a carefully worded missive in response when his work was interrupted by Akihiko's tweet. He paused from explaining to Jim that nicknames can be hurtful, and, worse, harmful to one's media persona and long-term career prospects, and were certainly never to be used in public without explicit prior permission of the one being nicked. Walker read Sato's retort to the Little Prince's impersonation of pitching predecessors.

These men deserve respect, not mockery. Let's respect baseball's history.

Respect

Sato followed this tweet with photographs of Tiant, Palmer, McGregor, and Quisenberry.

***

Moisés took a yellow cab to the ballpark. He was alone. He wanted to arrive well ahead of the team so that he could think through his plan for the game. The hotel was a den of confusion crawling with reporters and a few notorious Angels' fans who inserted themselves into the media kerfuffle over his managerial style. One jammed a cellphone in his face to record his response to the question: *retire now, old man*. He imagined a nearly empty visitor's clubhouse as a place of relative solace and peace.

He might have asked Jim if he could use Jim's office were that not so contrary to baseball custom.

Based on Jack's input, Moisés felt that he should shuffle his line-up, maybe even add a surprise starter. This wasn't how he knew the game to work, though. His instinct was to make no changes whatsoever. A game is a game, a loss is a loss. The key was to forget about it, to come to the ballpark the next day and do one's best to win the next game. That's what he had always been taught, and that's what he had always taught his men. *Short memories, gentleman.* That's what he told them yesterday at the truncated post-game team meeting. Short memories. Put this behind us. Tomorrow we face Sato.

***

Mrs. S. aged during the drive to the ballpark. She hadn't before looked so old, but now she was Mrs. Havisham steering a flaming wheelchair through heavier than usual traffic, cutting off imports and striking fear into a pedestrian mother of three fleeing CVS monopoly oppression. It must be hard since her husband, The Aged, vanished from her life. The Little Prince thought that Mrs. S. put on a good front, but he could tell she was bereaved at nearly every waking moment. Mrs. S. may have disliked baseball as much as he did, and yet there they were, conjoined sins, so different as to be nearly identical.

The Little Prince stared out the window and his mind wandered. He recalled a literary critic who told a story about a Parisian who so hated the *tour Eiffel* that he lunched there daily so that his gaze was spared its steely architecture. This thinking coincided with Mr. S.'s misshaped temple rising in Mrs. S.'s transparent windshield, blocking sunlight and rendering sepia long-established arcades and streetscapes.

***

The clubhouse player chairs were the stuff of legend. Leather of this quality began ice cold but melted with body heat, growing evermore supple as every pore delivered respiration. With the right body, these luxurious leather chairs moistened to the extent that they emitted fossil-blue smoke. Machetes were needed to free oneself.

Paul Bäumer, who last had a thought in his head before his peace and quiet was disturbed; Ole Paul might have sat himself in Alsace and put his feet on Lorraine. That young solider might have nearly disappeared into reverie, into a leathery trench, his sketchbook at his side. The Little Prince absolutely lived for such moments. Sinking into his own reverie, he began to spool out questions: does the cloud between my mind and me and me and the world represent accumulated falsehood. Is this question itself an illusion, the cloud but endogenous biomedical mass. Why does it cover my face rather than shield my calves. What would Paul Bäumer and Mike Flanagan say about that.

Soon enough, questions gave way to answers. The Little Prince lay in Jim's office. Green and blue glass shades were set yellowy aglow by New York Nineteenth Century Lower Tier manufacturers. His mind started to play tricks on him. He noticed that the locker room outside was preternaturally darkened and that a door had opened. A figure stole in the dark. He called out: who's there. Again, who is that. Terror rising. Who *is* it. Who is there. A guttural eruption began its journey, moving inexorably like an exploding gas from deep underground. Fear. Sound. Just then, Jim appeared. The boy awoke writhing and, although mostly failing in his attempt, trying to form words, to scream out. Jim's right hand provided direct pressure on the young soldier's arm. He stared down, his face shellshock. The Youth knew from that moment that Jim was his long-lost father.

Behind Jim stood Dave and Jeff. A minute previous, they had been satisfied that their plans were sound. This season was going to be interesting, Dave said. We're going to be able to periodically rest guys that we didn't know we were going to be able to periodically rest, added Jeff. Jim had been the only one of them to compose a classical period symphony of counterpoint and caution. He addressed the predictable distractions that were likely to be intense and interfering. He was dialed into how perverse raised expectations could be, and he cited the historical record, which he had researched recently, to argue that it's never good to imagine that any person can transcend a sport whose myth about itself was more than a century old. Tell Doubleday about *that*, Jim concluded emphatically, addressing a Generalized Other.

The crevasse between Jim's Hillary eyes and Norgay nose-bridge was proof of lifelong worrying that was sometimes mistaken for a youthful climbing accident. Jim worried that his neophyte pitcher might crash the new car he was sure to buy at the player's discount from Mrs. S. into the gated community in which he was sure to relocate under Mrs. S.'s steady supervision, or that he'd pay homage to Tommy John after one too many wicked breaking balls that he'd spin despite whether Jim had called for them (as he did begrudgingly). Jim worried that this wandering boy, so precious and precocious, would be struck down in a parking lot or go the way of The Spaceman. Worse, might he and Jim confront cannibals on the road from Knoxville to what was sold as salvation in post-apocalyptic Saint Pete.

Dave and Jeff listened as Jim drew air into his brightly lit Oval, one thinking it was early in the day for so much smoking and the other enjoying the light show. As he was making what seemed his ultimate point, Scooter interrupted with an update from the front office, and the tension evaporated as Jim cupped the phone to relay a flash from the one -man satellite communication hub that was Walker Evans Stefanski. Sad news, gentleman, but it seems that Earl has been struck by a toss during infield. From the direction of third. Oh my. Seems the ball located the man's pearls. Be a good lackey, Scooter, and check and see if this crime was caught on video. And let me be the first to declare that we shall hold whoever did this *accountable*. Mark my words, gentleman (now speaking to the bookshelf), I will have someone's baseballs in a sling for this. Jeff nodded in affirmation, but neither Scooter nor Dave offered even barest signs of life.

It was then that a cry rose up from the clubhouse. Jim led the way. The startled ingénue stared wide-eyed, with something that looked like chocolate smeared on his face and shirt, ankle mangled in a trap, voyageurs singing *Alouette, Gentille Alouette.*

SIX

When Jim was a boy, his adopted mother, an aunt, drove him to a K-Mart. The Murry Family was on vacation in Michigan, which was then the Winter Water Wonderland. Although he was young, Jim knew this wasn't the usual beach towels or tube socks drill. The Winter Water Wonderland was an enchanted place. Jim was pretty sure that the quarry they sought was an eight- or nine-foot tall World Series champion pitcher, one Mr. Mickey Lolich of Portland, Oregon. When they found him, Mr. Lolich stood next to a simple metal cart sculpted, as though by Koons, with dozens of pristine white baseballs. The balls were so new, so unadulterated, as to glow, while the gray cart aided contrast. A dull metallic post extended into the air and was crowned, as K-Mart liked to do in those days, with a flashing blue light that they had borrowed from a European police car or perhaps leased from Hawaii Five-O. This signaled a Blue Light Special. Usually a discount on skin cream or underwear, today the blue light summoned shoppers to meet a real-life hero.

For a few cash-dollars, one of the Game's Greats would select a ball from the basket, ink his signature, and bend at the waist, bringing his bluest porcelain blue eyes low. Mr. Lolich would carefully inspect the presented elfin creature. Discerning the contours of its nascent soul with a penetrating diamond-tested gaze, Mr. Lolich would then smile and place one Fabergé egg into the hesitant outstretched hand of a future memory. Lolich could not have known, his palm slathered, presumably, with a paucity of grease, that he would inspire a future big leaguer who would go on to become manager of perhaps the greatest pitcher to play the game.

What would Mickey Lolich think of that, Jim wondered. Reminiscing was one of Jim's favorite activities and he indulged it more and more. Jim enjoyed the freedom of free association, how one thought led to another. The thought of Lolich sparked a second: the trio of Lolich, Denny McClain, and Bob Gibson. Jim surmised that his fresh-faced ace might be a combination of Lolich's goodness, McClain's badness, and Gibson's heroism. Jim had known this lad for all of six weeks; less than a week had passed since the kid had burst into most people's consciousness. That wasn't much time for The Great Unwashed, perhaps, but six weeks was plenty of time for Jim to daydream about Mickey Lolich, a trip to Rome, boyhood epiphanies, Dr. King, Virginia Beach, English Ovals, Mark "The Bird" Fidrych, and The Great Willie Horton.

***

The White Sox appeared in throw-back black. Black hats, jerseys, pants, shoes and sox. Grey-white trim. Monochrome delight. But Jim and Jeff and Dave also spied what they thought might be a little red and green and yellow radiating from Sox hitters, pitchers, coaches, management representatives, not to mention pesky TV broadcasters.

We're no Angels, you know what I mean, Jim.

Truly, the breaking balls and location were more impressive than the heat.

Damn it all, Jeff, we broke our best pitching machine because of that kid.

But can you keep his head on straight, that's what I wonder. Good luck with that.

How are you managing distractions. It's a circus. *Carnival.* Man, it's gotta be fun.

***

Having never pitched in the majors—or any professional baseball game, any competently officiated baseball game with nine on each side—Mrs. S.'s Little Prince had no idea what to do between starts. Consequently, and under direct orders from Jim, the Little Prince and Jeff were to be inseparable during the final two games with the Angels and the entire forthcoming three-game series with the White Sox. This was the root of Jim's distinctive approach to *manège*: people and their emotions first. The Little Prince was first asked to closely observe and subsequently analyze Sato's outing against the still-reeling Angels, but there wasn't much to see or unpack or dutifully report. Sato was magnificent. He struck out eight, walked two, scattered five hits (all harmless singles), was never threatened, was always in command, and was relieved in the ninth with a 5-0 lead. Sanchez came on in relief and gave up a towering home run into the centerfield fountains before managing the final out, but, all agreed, it was a superb pitching performance all around.

An incident occurred after the game. Sato returned from the interview room wearing an especially inscrutable expression. He walked straight toward the kid, barely acknowledging a smattering of that-a-boys. When he was within two feet, looming overhead, Akihiko Sato said in near-perfect American English: Yankees are either General LeMay or Robert McNamara. Which are you, *boy*. The silence between them grew to envelop the clubhouse's southeast quadrant. Constable Jeff of the Stefanski-Murry nanny state appeared and formed a triad. Sato repeated his seemingly intemperate question: which are you. Jim appeared and interceded. He felt he knew exactly what was at stake: it was a question about pilots and intellectuals and places. It might as well have concerned Arras or Dresden or Hanoi. Henry Kissinger's jowly face invaded Jim's take on the Paris Peace Talks before him. *Le garçon* grew or remained stoic and mute, late arrivers couldn't tell which. Jim saw the cultural divide between them, the cultural lag and culture shock. In such delicate matters, stoic and mute was the right call, Jim thought.

***

Carlson pitched the third and last game of the series against the Angels. He followed history and excellence with an Ole Miss B. Not that he was an alumnus. Hugh "Carly" Carlson had passed on college stateside for a league education in Korea and Japan. Hugh fell in love with, and, truth be told, *in* each country, his return to the U.S. for a coveted major league roster position bittersweet as a result. Having thrown sixty-five pitches and unable to use any of those to secure an out in the third, Jim pulled Carly with two Angels across and three on base, a dubious but, Jim acknowledged, all too common full house. Carly donned a hair shirt and fireman rushed in where Angels feared not to tread. Against steep odds, the home team nonetheless rallied to win a third straight. Television was dizzy with their fever, and three games into the season, even the West Wing communication office made a play for electoral hay. Zephyr quipped to his wife that, with so much publicity, they were the town of the talk.

***

Lucy would be fifteen, but she had always been a born researcher. She rued the bad luck that left her the daughter of an era without easy recourse to card catalogues, microfiche, and vertical files. Lucy would have thrived as apprentice to a Royal Society librarian. Indeed, her soulmate, on whom she pined, was Oxford's James Macie-Smithson. Sans alternatives, Lucy used modern conveniences and contrivances in a quest to profile a ballplayer on whose head the media had laid bounty. She averred: I am in this for myself. Lucy did not wish to engage this rare specimen, who sooner or later she could not avoid, without proper prior investigation. What if he were a loquacious advocate for antidisestablishmentarianism. Or, worse, she said, a lulu.

***

Dr. Mary Sweetwater obliged her father and provided him conversation. Mary happily performed her duties as a prescribed chauffeur and nursemaid. All dad needed was a lift from his modest urban elite neighborhood to his office in the medical arts building near the research hospital. Every city has one or more such neighborhoods, professional enclaves close to anchor institutions that boast perceptible racial and ethnic diversity and opportunity for the bourgeois *flâneur* to saunter old-timey sidewalks. Every such city also enjoys a smattering of professional office buildings of the sort that Mary's dad called home. Mary knew that she grew up in her dad's local Bauhaus as much as she did in the aging two-story Tudor with detached garage and thinning ivy.

Dad, you're not being a good patient. I was there when Gloria told you to take it easy for a week or two, preferably a lifetime. You'll recall I was the hundred and twenty-pound spider in the corner.

I'm not driving.

Not-driving is not following doctor's orders, dear father.

I taught you better than that.

It is wordplay, dad.

I mean about work. I have much to do. People rely on us. Life and death.

You don't have to remind me. I lost a patient yesterday.

I'm sorry. A tough case.

I didn't think so. A boy. Something genetic, I think.

They'll let you know.

The parents were stoic. They thanked me, stood, and left.

I've had that happen. There are so many Amish and Mennonite....

No, they were both teachers, at the same school. Here in town, I think.

You know there is a tough case I'm working on. It's Margie.

You're treating Margie.

No. She asked me to look at some film. A second opinion.

Dad, you shouldn't do that. And you don't need me to tell you why.

It's Margie. I wanted to help. If it's what she thinks and what I think it is, I will help her make an appointment at Mayo, MD Anderson. She shouldn't hesitate.

Or Hopkins.

I think it's bad, Mary. Her brainstem

What does she know.

She knows that her team is fast out of the gate and that Alek wouldn't want her to miss this opportunity to do something good.

I thought Margie was bottom-line.

She is, but because she wants to do something good with the money. She and Alek had that wish. Maybe it was his wish more than hers, but it's hers now, too.

***

Juan-Luis García opened the three-game series with the Sox by shutting them down for six innings. Regrettably for Juan-Luis, his excellent pitching coincided with his team's offense taking a few innings off to enjoy soothing beaches in the Lesser Antilles. No sooner had this cynicism crossed Juan-Luis' mind than all hell broke loose in the seventh and rendered past tense the game's previous zero-to-zero tie. Juan-Luis got the first two Sox hitters to fly out to St. Peter's and St. Paul's, respectively, but a two-out hit followed by a four-ball walk had Jim and Jeff in a staring contest. Jeff broke away to step near to the Little Prince, who was not supposed to be reading fiction other than the respected novel entitled, *Scouting Report*, nor listening, as he was, to something called *The Orwells*. Jeff hand-signaled and then surreptitiously whispered *pay close attention*. Working from the stretch, Garcia checked the runner, without first asking permission, with a soft throw. Jim had delegated this authority, a vote of confidence in Juan-Luis.

Garcia looked in and grooved a fastball belt-high to Whit Mueller. Whit, everyone knew, was again leading the league in home runs. True to form, he splashed Juan-Luis' next meek offering into Belgium's champagne shoreline. Jeff appeared at the mound to ask Juan-Luis how he felt, and, particularly, if he was feeling as though he might give up another bomb to right field. Juan-Luis' candid reply came instead from left-field: I don't like that kid reading while I'm pitching. I don't like it. *Make him stop*. Make him stop.

Juan-Luis spit something in Spanish, a gesture caught on television, as he passed The Amazing Read-O-Matic before ducking down the tunnel to recover his lost equanimity. The Sox would have won the game had they not given up seven runs in the seventh, a Fukushima Daiichi meltdown that sent the home crowd on a two-week all-expense paid what-happens-there-stays-there vacation, kids packed off to *obaasan*.

***

Scooter Libby had never been so busy. Dave was cracking the whip and Scooter was enthralled. Most of the front office was, in contrast, comparatively staid. They were mainly old-school baseball people. They had seen streaks of both types result in nothing one way or the other. Jim didn't hold their detachment against them. He didn't affirm it. He didn't celebrate it as evidence of maturity or balance. But he didn't criticize it either. He recalled Mary Daly: to each *bore-a-crat* his own, he muttered to himself.

In spite of the four-game winning streak, Jim hadn't laughed in days.

The thought of a baseball manager quoting a radical feminist theorist the likes of Mary Daly incited in him mild yet noticeable chuckling. His centerfielder asked him to explain himself and Jim uttered something about Starhawk and feminist neopaganism. His increasingly puzzled and then increasingly concerned interlocutor heard his manager buckling under the immense pressure of early season success and the near-continuous scrutiny of Kid Phenom. He knew that Jim had been quizzed endlessly on the kid's nearly non-existent baseball résumé, to which Jim had made routine yet unsatisfactory allusion to the precedents of Gates Brown and Ron LeFlore. *We got this*, Harold Morris assured his skipper. Hey, he said, peering into Jim's eyes and with a firm internationally acclaimed hand on Jim's shoulder, we got this. Jim returned Harold's gaze and was embarrassed to only now realize that his especially fleet centerfielder was powered by a human heart.

***

Dan and Maria Higgins were immensely proud of their Fouled Ball Girl. Lucy's foul-ling—a neologism that Lucy coined and that Maria, not entirely inaccurately, believed referred to Lucy's online peeps who tweeted her—had increased ten-fold since the season had gotten underway. Lucy was independent, always doing something without her parents' direct involvement, and they, her parents, wanted to show their support by joining her for a game early in the season. As challenging as it was, the Higgins' scrapped together all available liquid assets by sweeping balances from various accounts dedicated to deferred maintenance needs and rainy days. This ransom in hand, they purchased a wheelchair-accessible and companion ticket and made detailed plans in confession-like conference with team fan-experience experts. The Higgins' then began to prepare mentally for Thursday's game against the Sox.

When they finally arrived at them, their seats were located so high down the leftfield line that Lucy couldn't even pretend to see them; it was their punishment, Maria assumed, for having asked for extra consideration. But a foul ball or two might come their way, she thought. If so, a fouled ball might be a special gift to share with Lucy.

Maria knew more about baseball than did Dan because her father had played in school as well as with a community team in Mexico. He even pitched. It's too bad, she thought, that Lucy's grandfather lived halfway across the continent. He would have enjoyed seeing her take her place on the field. Maria's reportage would be poor substitute for seeing Lucy on the pitch, in full radiant command of the leftfield line.

Dan was exhausted by the journey from home to stadium. He suffered through what felt like an equal distance from the initial frisk-down to arrival, after three separate elevator rides, at K2's oxygen-deprived leftfield summit. It was so high that he looked to see if he could glimpse Tibet's Lake Yamdrok but instead caught his first taste of wind. Dan didn't swear or complain. He never did. His body could be covered in carbuncles and he would no sooner give voice to his pain and sorrow as drive his wheelchair off the Golden Gate Bridge. He and Maria held hands and tried to keep one another warm. Even though they hadn't accounted for exposure to straight winds or the chill after loss of direct sunlight, they were happy. Lucy was their diamond girl refracting klieg lights.

***

Jason J. Ueberroth was Jim and Jeff's fourth starter. At least, that had been the plan coming out spring training. When Mrs. Stefanski showed up one day a few weeks before the opening with a starting pitcher in tow, Jason didn't know it, but he was going to be moved one spot down the pecking order and Chet Smith was leaving the dugout for the bullpen. Both pitchers, it turned out, were instrumental in a fifth straight win, Jay by getting into trouble in the first inning, and Smitty by coming on to save the inning as well as warm the Higgins' and their forty thousand fellow climbers' frigid cold evening.

The White Sox jumped all over Jason's primary pitches. There was plenty of contact, including the Sox fouling off more than a few. Lucy made a play for one particularly hard-hit ball down the line, but it skipped over her shoulder into the seats. Her parents were ecstatic: Lucy appeared momentarily on the mammoth centerfield screen. Unfortunately, because she was scrupulously attending to business, Lucy missed her point-five seconds of fame. Laced fouls soon straightened into line drives.

People forget, Jeff would explain: an expansive outfield keeps the number of homers down, but it means that pitchers are bound to issue more singles, doubles, and triples. Jay gave up one of each, two walks and a wild pitch as well. He left the game before any number of fans could be one-hundred percent certain that what they had been watching were pitches that count. Smitty was in a groove the rest of the evening. He even finished the game. His offense bailed Jason and him out by scoring two runs each in the fifth, sixth, seventh, and eighth. The team was gelling, Jim had to concede.

**

Preparation for his second start involved sitting and watching other people play baseball. That's what Jim and Jeff wanted, and Dave backed them. Just take it easy. Jesus, enough with the books. Read the scouting report. You have. Well, read it again.

In truth, there were arm and shoulder exercises and some jogging. But no throwing. No discussion of pitching. And no talking with the media. The last was a priority. To keep things on the down-low, Mrs. S. and Jeff took turns chauffeuring The Little Prince to and from *Le Shantytown* and *Stade de Stefanski*. It was during this time when Mrs. S. was first introduced to Jim's office's secret entrance, which she took in stride. In fact, having seen evidence of paparazzi, it was Mrs. S. herself who hired a double to impersonate her ward by driving his petit fire engine around the city before arriving at a luxury hotel. This was good work for the faux freshman imposter, who was paid by the hour as he slept, belly round on room service and minifridge. Even though his inaccessibility exacerbated media frothing, the Little Prince was glad for this bubble.

***

Hector, since last week's opening miracle, we have looked forward to this day.

Seth, I am with you. So excited for today. I want to see history again, my man.

***

As regular Free Press *readers know, this observer shares none of the newfound enthusiasm for perfection which some seem to regard as the sport's second coming. I appreciate the honesty involved in what we have seen, the untutored, unmanaged, free and authentic expression of baseball virtuosity. It's not unlike, I suppose, a cheetah in full flight or a condor surprising its prey. Every once in a blue moon, the extreme edges of things deserve our undivided attention, if for no other reason that the better we gauge that which is relatively commonplace. For me, I enjoyed Sato's outing more than any of his teammates'. Enjoyed, I stress. I value competition and contest as well as excellence. Sato's game offered the right balance for my baseball pallet. The White Sox hope to avoid a sweep tonight, and all eyes will be on our artificially lit Phenom. My guess is that our side shall prevail, but so, too, shall baseball. Prediction: Perfection: 0, Sox: Minus 2.*

***

If I were Jim Murry, I would quit. Let's face it: Ole Jim's been to the mountaintop and there is only downside in every direction. Once a team has experienced pure perfection, everything else pales. The News *has provided me this privileged perch for more years than I care to acknowledge, but if I ever write the perfect column, that will be the last you hear from me. Unfortunately, I am nothing like tonight's Beethoven, Brahms, and Bach rolled into one. You may rest assured, therefore, that I will be back in this space after the game to share perspective on the result of tonight's historic test of mettle. If you want to know what I think going in, here it is: The* White Sox *are busting at every seam of every baseball, ready to burst our bubble as they blast out of their recent hitting slump. Sorry fans, you can't win them all, even when you have such remarkable raw talent on your side. The odds favor the Sox. But who really knows what will happen.*

***

The prohibition against talking with the media extended to listening, reading, emailing, and texting with the media, or anyone who lived next door to the media. Newspapers and radios were barred from the clubhouse. Televisions that Dave controlled from his office featured cooking and house-swap shows. Sammy mumbled that Guy Fieri must have been added to the roster, but no one seemed to mind these minor inconveniences. With their unexpected start and superstar-in-the-making, there was goodwill aplenty. Like Juan-Luis' expressed frustration, Sato's enigmatic tweet and locker room explosion seemed faint turbulence within a new general air of excitement.

The absence of reality television conflict helped Jim cope with things. Scooter strongly favored more action and more news. But Dave was convinced that a calm front office and bubbly clubhouse mood redounded to his leadership. Jeff instinctively aided Jim, while Jim kept eyes peeled for signs of anarchy: actionable, philosophical, or both.

In spite of vigilance, there was no way to avoid what Jim called baseball's *bro*mides, what he prosaically termed its bull. Ninety-five percent of the time when people in the professional baseball ranks interacted with one another, it was through bromides. Not Harold Morris, who looked him in the eye and told him everything was going to be all right; that was a five-percent experience. Not when Jim, Jeff, and Dave had comforted the kid after his nightmare. But most of the time. Baseball's daily bromides would have probably drove Jim out long ago had he not acquired managerial authority, an office sanctuary, and a late-in-life love for reading the books he wished he had read more of when in high school. When Mr. S. stocked his endless bookshelves, Jim was grateful from the bottom of his heart. The first book that he selected to read from this miraculous bounty was about a boy and his dad written by James Agee.

***

Home whites versus visitors in chic ebony and jet onyx. Manichean, or so observed the single instance of *homo sapiens* in either cave who stood a better than even chance of accurately defining Manichean. He said this with enough wavelength energy as to propagate it in his teammates' acoustical range. Several looked at him, including Sato. The Little Prince discerned that the word Manichean furthered their distance rather than landed a connection. How cliché, he followed. Still no response, although now his teammates read one another's faces for where this was going. Okay, let's not start the silent treatment before the game even begins, he offered.

Jeff sat. Remember our game plan. We are going to go with fastballs, with a few breaking balls to keep them honest. Throw strikes and we'll be fine. Famous last words thought tonight's would-be flamethrower. Throw it where they most expect it. *Good plan.*

The walk to the mound took eight or nine seconds. During these eight or nine seconds, tonight's starting pitcher reflected on several pressing issues. He had some sense of why Mrs. S. tolerated his living quarters, but he didn't understand why Jeff hadn't been more alarmed. Jeff sat for a minute at his kitchen table, enough time for him to finish a story about a tough stint in Arkansas—maybe it was Hot Springs. The tenant of Teenage Squalor Court wasn't sure exactly what happened to Jeff in Arkansas and didn't have time to listen carefully because he was busy clearing the top of his chest of drawers. The Little Prince again acknowledged that it didn't make sense to throw fastballs over the plate when the opposition had surely prepared for exactly that.

Jim and Jeff asked him politely not to take interpretive license with the signs: *just throw fastballs when we tell you to throw fastballs.* The Little Prince decided, his feet touching the mound, to say to himself what he was feeling daily and what was pressing on him especially at that very moment. His parents left him for dead. The Little Prince knew this meant he was unworthy, perhaps worthless. Why else would they have died and made him continue to live. Certain of his own impending death, and, to an extent, welcoming of it, the Little Prince wasn't sure he would make it through the first inning. And now that he was high on the mound, he wasn't sure he could launch a first pitch, let alone a second. Why didn't Jim or any adult understand his denials as a form of denial. You've got an adolescent crying out, literally, and your best solution is *Jeff Millsaps.*

***

Play ball!

***

The stadium was ubiquitous blue magical sparkle and orange crush musical flash. The

Little Prince was the wilting star of a rustbelt Main Street Electrical Parade.

***

Sammy put down the sign for a two-seam fastball, preferably knee-high and on the edge of home plate Umpire Zach Linville's zone. Amid a mad torrent of thunder and lightning, the gill-packed leaned in for a superior view of history or his-story or both.

The Sox leadoff hitter, Nelson Ruiz, caught enough of the 90-mile per hour elevated speedball to redirect it square into Sammy's facemask. Because the laws of physics had returned to their normal Earth complement, the facemask proceeded to collide with Sammy's head like a jab in the face from a well-lathered Muhammad Ali. A stiff punch would be bad enough for a sparring partner or well-compensated marquee opponent, but for the unsuspecting Sammy Robertson, it was a knock-out blow. Sammy staggered three steps before melting. Linville leaped to mitigate Sammy's rapid loss of composure. Umpires as well as trainers from both dugouts converged on the limp body. The crowd, moments prior set to explode, fizzled and smoldered instead. They were clutching a carousel that suddenly lurched and halted, its riders waved off to the side.

***

Nine minutes passed while Sammy received attention. Precaution required that he leave on a stretcher, a policy that he barely protested. The starting pitcher, ahead 0 and 1, stood behind the mound and toyed with his thoughts. He was aware of Sammy's situation but there was nothing he could do except get in the way of those who knew what to do. He cared that Sammy recover, fully and quickly, but he could hear snippets from first and second to the contrary. The ball felt cold in his hands and he thought he might be sick to his stomach. He tossed it into his glove as a kid does who's trying to take his mind off something, but for many players and spectators, he was George Herbert Walker Bush checking his watch. Many of those who last week had been pinned down next to him on Iwo Jima, their individual odds of surviving the beach as miniscule as his odds of escaping twenty-seven batters without contact, were now clearing brush with flamethrowers and paving B-29 runways with heavy equipment.

***

Eugene Morgan Smith replaced Samuel Kenneth Robertson. Gene was a good guy, but he warmed up with third baseman, Scott Winters, and said nothing to his pitcher. The first time he made eye-contact was when he flashed the next sign: four-seam fastball, inside. Ruiz fouled that one off as well. A game transpired last week without contact, but this week, it was as though yin was yang and karma had come 'round. The third pitch was outside, off the plate. Ruiz swung through it and cursed.

The Ruiz at-bat was a microcosm for the game. Balls were fouled every which way, including into the far upper leftfield deck near where the Dan and Maria sat two nights previous. Lucy didn't field any herself, but she did watch as Sox batter after batter lined balls all over the park, but to striding and diving and leaping outfielders. The infield was similarly active. Over their several chances, they never bobbled a ball or sent an errant throw. It was a defensive clinic. Put-outs became increasingly dramatic as the game progressed. Leaps at the wall competed with diving infield stabs. Ruiz's strikeout was one of only two through seven innings, the other a checked swing called on appeal.

Sox batters had done their homework. They sat on fastballs and made level contact. Despite countless line-drives in play, they were, however, hitless heading into the eighth. What's more, Zimmerman's solo moonshot meant that they were behind one run to zero. The Sox had kicked their heels all over Jim's forty acres, but they had nothing on the scoreboard to show for it. They were down to their final six at-bats: six men facing a lashing typhoon water wall, a wildly unpredictable blue and orange wave.

***

For her own amusement more than for the delight of first-row spectators, Lucy chose the seventh inning to dub tonight's starting pitcher a would-be No-No Nanette. This quip elicited a smirk from a gentleman nearing ninety-three, and a disbelieving stare from his seventy-five-year-old daughter-caregiver. For Lucy, the Little Prince was a flapper gloriously enjoying independence while only by necessity husbanding marital eligibility. He might as well be a dizzy dame, she thought, the way he's pitching; he certainly appeared to be traversing a narrowing balance beam. In any case, the always grounded Fouled Ball Girl expected some kind of comical falling out.

***

The Little Prince walked the first two batters in the eighth inning. His breaking balls started out of the zone and fooled no one by staying there. The third batter, Ethan Hillsborough, moved the baserunners over with a sacrifice down the first base line. The pitcher fled the mound, cleanly fielded the spinning sphere, and made a confident throw to erase Hillsborough. The Little Prince surprised himself with the feat. But the momentum wasn't going his way. The field began to tilt against him. As he walked slowly back to the mound, he looked burdened and in need of relief. The noise was too much for him. The air pressure was weighing him down.

Next came the Sox's best batting average with teammates in scoring position. The Little Prince walked Monsieur Contact Hitter on four straight pitches. Jim concluded that none of the pitches showed any stomach for the dish, that his starting pitcher was afraid to give up a bomb, that his miraculous flying machine was out of gas. That impression—not the over-capacity rumblings emanating from an overwrought peanut gallery—freed the team's skipper from his hold. Jim emerged from the dugout with a raised arm for Jacob Williams. Frère Jacques, he sang, let us gather in prayer.

Gene was first to the mound. Before Jim arrived, he spit Cobra venom into his pitcher's eyes. It wasn't right that a pitcher wouldn't check on the condition of his catcher, especially, the way Gene saw it, since it was a cross-up that felled Sammy.

***

Seth, I am surprised. I admit it. I'm shocked.

I think it has to do with Robertson's injury.

Right. Here's a guy, a young and inexperienced guy, who, despite the obvious struggle tonight, is leaving the game with a no-hitter intact. Man, oh man. Backing up an incredible perfect game with a no-hitter through eight. And there's a smattering of boos.

I think not just from the fans, Hector.

What we saw from Smith at the mound.

Yes, and what we're seeing in the dugout.

What have you done for me lately. I have no words, man.

Jake Williams is jogging in from the bullpen, Hector.

I don't get it, Seth. He didn't do anything but what he was asked to do.

SEVEN

Darrell's Bar & Grill had been in continuous operation since the last millennium, which Darrell thought more impressive sounding than in business since one score and seven years ago. Specialties of the house included 'burgers and homemade fries, cheese steak, and chicken fingers, although not a few regulars also sucked on pickled baloney and pickled vegetables and brought their families for the bi-weekly fish fries. Darrell liked to use butter, mayonnaise, and healthy amounts of gravy and cheese. His popular cheese fries with gravy and a mayonnaise dipping sauce were but an example of the extent of this proclivity. Health inspectors rated him highly but refused samples.

Mr. Reginald and Mr. Reggie Ross shared a familial bond and a corner table. Reggie thought it provided the best view of Darrell's large-size projection television, but Mr. Ross was skeptical. Normally, given the hour, they would be at their respective dwellings mixing combinations of bubbly aluminum, magnesium, and calcium carbonate if having patronized Darrell's previously. Ross the Elder thought it funny that the fix for stomach troubles were rare earth metal cocktails. He and Reggie were eager to join the world to watch if history would repeat itself. There were no empty seats or stools. Effervescent celebration pulsed through the front and sounded off through Darrell's rear, a veritable vespertine digest of the Ross neighborhood organic *conscience collective*.

Reggie had been popping since the start but was particularly demonstrative once the third inning rolled around. He couldn't help but be influenced by his environment and the cold brews that kept coming. Reggie worked the edges of his seat like the starting pitchers groped for the corners of the plate. He dined on butter-fried potato drizzled with fat and coagulated beef juice and ate hungrily as his hero fed Sox batters juicy outfield flies and assorted pop-up cookies. A spill in the seventh wasn't addressed until the stretch, and trips to the restroom were more common than commercial breaks. Reggie never had so much fun. He told anyone who would listen that he and his co-pilot had rescued the struggling Phenom from on-ramp hesitation and possible self-destruction.

***

The elder Ross looked at Reggie and smiled, but instead of thinking happy thoughts about Reggie and baseball, Mr. Ross involuntarily recalled the American Indo-China War. Drafted out from under his family, Pvt. Willard K. Ross, or Willie, lasted two days out of Saigon. Mr. Ross suspected that his kid brother, ten years his junior, was a pacifist with a death wish. Mr. Ross remembered that Willie cried himself silent after learning that his number was up. His tendency to roll and moan automatically in his sleep lessened noticeably before he shipped out. The Greatest of All Time and he shared a feeling that no one *over there*—over there having lost its dough boy patina, its showbiz dung coating—nobody over there had ever done him no harm. Unlike The Champ, however, Willie had no nation to which to turn. Like Ali, it was the nation itself that was suffocating him, compelling Willie into a spiral of contradiction. Willie's body, Mr. Ross recalled, was discovered broken and twisted in a supply truck's front axle, an unfortunate accident, said the Army Coroner's Report, along the way to his own Dien Bien Phu.

***

That afternoon's flight through the city required Mrs. S. to remind herself that she was driving the car. She had been around baseball long enough to know that there was no such thing as an undefeated season. A loss would not trouble her. In fact, she hoped a loss might simmer things down, including Mayor Laundry. It was Sam who was distracting her presently. Margie had mistakenly taken a call. He began with a little baseball small talk. It seemed to Sam unavoidable, and, in any case, he chose not to pursue an alternative. Margie and he moved as manners allowed to the purpose for the call, which was to share recommendations that included Sam's preferred clinic in Minnesota and something pat about the Texas Medical Center. She now stood amid an owner's box pre-game celebration, Earl and Walker talking turns singing into the other's ear. *This couldn't wait*, Sam had implored. He was apologetic but determined. Margie touched her phone. Zephyr caught her eye and raised a toast from across the universe.

***

Jim missed a beat as he entered his office, seeing his losing pitcher stretched-out on his leather rack. Jim's office was in but not of the clubhouse, he liked to think. Players and coaches and members of the media cycled through, as they should, but he expected that they should do so dressed in Eastern Clothing Company suits and ties, Chuck Daly's outfitter, or at least something from Filene's Basement. If accents included French cuffs, Italian leather shoes, and monographed whatever, that was fine with Jim. Mr. S. had provided a tastefully decorated locker room and lavish training room, the modest disrepair of latter more cosmetic than functional. The kid should be deep in a stainless-steel whirlpool or having Ed Rollins massage his shoulder, which apparently needed something like a Rollins massage to restore its strength and luster.

Or, he should be dressed and waiting on Mrs. S. He should not be laying on Jim's couch.

Jim put his embarrassing pettiness behind him as fast as it took him to see the boy's tears. Jeff already knew. It was he who insisted on Jim's couch, and it was he who slipped into the office behind Jim and lowered the blinds. This was a Do Not Disturb sign not easily misread by baseball players accustomed to interpreting the meanings of the smallest things: bat-flips, pregnant pauses, akimbo poses, empty suits, empty seats.

I've called Margie.

Okay.

She's going to meet us at the parking lot and get this guy home tonight.

Okay.

Jim, I think we should reconsider this whole thing.

Why.

This is a lot to handle. That crowd tonight was…Holy Mary, Mother of God.

I know.

Jim, we need to talk with Dave. He doesn't see what we see. Margie, too.

Mrs. Stefanski knows.

I will tell you what Margie doesn't *want* to know. Junior here has a history of addiction issues. He should be tested every day, week, and month.

The BPA requires that.

It does, but he's not been tested yet.

What's wrong with him.

Jim, it's more the case of what's *not* wrong with him.

Jeff, may I ask how you know all this.

I talked with people. He gave me permission.

This isn't PED stuff.

The opposite. What he has done would kill me or you. He cuts himself, too.

I don't know what you mean.

Kid, why don't you tell him. Jim's your manager. He ought to know.

***

Darrell's place was seven-eighths men, the few women present either in Darrell's employ, wandering aimlessly through life, or both. Mr. Ross always noted this and said a prayer for the world's womenfolk. From a young age, he recognized that if a space alien came down to Earth, no alien could fail to notice that menfolk ruled the world. Stevie Wonder was a blind black man, but he ruled the world. Donald Trump stunk like the ass-end of a city bus, but he ruled the world. Charlie Manson was universally reviled, but thanks to Quentin Tarantino, even in death he ruled the world. Jesus, Buddha, Muhammad, and the Pope, they all ruled the world too. There were exceptions. Mrs. Margaret Stefanski owned the team to which he had devoted a lifetime's devotion, but she inherited it from her husband, so Mr. Ross wasn't sure if she ruled the world. His holiness, The Dali Lama, Mr. Ross wasn't sure that he ruled the world either. Reggie was a good guy. He was polite to women and girls as he was to men and boys. But Mr. Ross wasn't sure if Reggie understood how privileged he was, a poor black dude from the fourth or fifth worst neighborhood in a beat down and drug out American city.

***

Let's take stock, Hector. We suffered our first loss of the season. Took a defense-oriented no-hitter into the eighth but Jake Williams couldn't contain a red-hot Sox line-up. His consolation is that all three of those Sox runs were unearned.

Seth, you're right, J.W. pitched his best but the Sox were poised to feast on anything around the plate. The big story, though, is the wild ride from tonight's starter.

Let's dissect his outing.

Oh man, the change from the first game to this game was dramatic. No acting out there. No submarine pitches, no knuckleballs. Just fastballs. One after the other. I didn't count but maybe five or ten breaking balls the whole night and none of them were much good. Still, the defense was spectacular. We've seen about everything, Seth.

My post-mortem is a little different than yours. What I saw was a young man taken off his game by what happened to Sammy Robertson on the game's first pitch.

You're right about that, Seth. It was like a curse. Everything seemed to change.

I can't recall seeing an injury cause such a change in mood or performance. We've seen some bad moments. But Robertson, I wasn't sure he was getting up.

I hear you, Seth. It was awful. But that don't explain all those fastballs and most all of them double digit. Compared to his debut, man, his pitches lacked giddy-up.

They did.

And so did *he*, Seth.

***

Dave began to embrace the intrigue that Margie started, and because Dave showed modest enthusiasm, it was impossible to keep Scooter off his leg. Dave and Scooter and Imposter #2 (Imposter #1 having been fired with extreme prejudice for bringing unauthorized guests to his hotel room) talked in a circle, pretending to be in deep discussion. The point was to do this while visible at the main security gate outside of the clubhouse, and then extend breadcrumbs to Imposter #2's upgraded vehicle, a Stefanski Motors black Escalade from the loaner collection. A team hoodie thwarted prying telescopic lenses: this was Scooter's only adopted idea. Dave had inspected the hotel and taken the opportunity to spread walking around money to management and staff. After what had happened with Imposter #1, which resulted in Kroger aisle tabloid stories, Dave decided to open the purse for security, bribery, and for his peace of mind.

Having once tried and failed to recreate in Nashville the chase scene from *Bullitt* (the ill-advised attempt to reincarnate Steve McQueen an equally spectacular wreck), Scooter worked to convince Dave that he had extensive VIP-driving experience and was certified by an executive protection firm in Virginia, the name of which he was prohibited from disclosing. Hence it was that Imposter #2's rendezvous with his hotel suite was delayed that night by Scooter's certainty that, A, they were being followed by a conspiracy of alternating motorcycles, and B, the way to lose this tail was to appear to detour across the river but, while still on the bridge, slash across lanes of on-coming traffic and double-back from whence they came. Imposter #2 was an un-bonded amateur imposter. Upon increasingly sober reflection, Imposter #2 declared that he would not be party to any such a demented suicide pack. After a call to Dave from the Escalade's state-of-the-art communication console, Imposter #2 was duly authorized to, A, leave the gun, and, B, to secure W. E. Stefanski Protective Services, Inc.'s cannoli.

***

Mrs. S. thought she glimpsed her nephew and passenger's doppelgänger speeding recklessly past at an intersection, but instead of welcoming the chance to make their bail she kept her mind on the road ahead. As they passed beneath an underpass, Mrs. S. realized that her fare wasn't faring well. It had been heartbreaking to watch him pour himself out. She thought it poignant that he was afraid to go on the road with the team. He kept begging to be allowed to stay in town. He didn't want to fly to Seattle and then on to Beantown and Baltimore. He wanted nothing more, he said, than to listen to music, hang-out with some friends, maybe watch a show. He specifically referenced something called *Bojack Horseman*, about which Mrs. S. feared the worst.

He said that, under the right circumstances, he might tackle the Appalachian Trial or set his sights on Rocky Mountain National Park. He spoke of his need to eat like a human, which confused everyone but Mrs. S. and Jeff, who had seen his kitchen. He talked about his desire to earn a university degree but was consumed with career interests in law enforcement, social work, and pharmacology. With dried tears matted to his blotchy swollen face, he had sat up in Jim's office and in a clear, sober voice said that, with help and in due time, he wanted to try and recapture the glory of his youth.

Now he was again weeping.

Honey, I want you to listen to me. You don't have to reply, just listen.

When I met you in Syracuse, I saw my husband as the young man who I never knew. I mean by that that I saw in you Alek's incredible intelligence, his drive to do what was right, but in you, I saw this as inchoate, you understand, as not fully developed. For my Alek, smart and good were not different things. You understand this, don't you.

I know that smart and good are not different things.

Right. That's what he believed. He never did anything for only one reason.

We *make* them different.

Pardon.

We force this difference into the world. We make it. We jam it down our own throats.

What is *it*, dear.

I don't know. The diremption of the soul.

What does that mean, sweetie. Who jams what down our throats.

Everyone and no one.

That's confusing.

Das Man.

Pardon me.

I guess it's untranslatable.

***

Mr. Ross the Elder didn't know Jim Murry but shared with him growing affection for nostalgia. Mr. Ross recalled his alma mater, Lawrenceville Senior High School. Lawrenceville's teachers were splendid, he thought. Mr. Ross was not supposed to attend a semi-rural school like Lawrenceville but the volatile circumstances of his city upbringing being what they were, his high school days occurred in the next county over living on what amounted to defunct farmland. In those days, high school was serious business. Trigonometry, American Literature, Biology, Chemistry, and, for a handful of students like Reginald, Physics and Psychology mixed with baseball and QWERTY.

Those were the days. *Teachers didn't play*, thought Mr. Ross. No, sir. They made sure he knew his B.F. Skinner, his Harlow Monkeys, his Margaret Mead; that made sure Mr. Ross would remember Isaiah Newton and Madame Currie. What they wouldn't teach, though, was anything about being black in this U.S. of A. That they sure wouldn't do, said Mr. Ross to himself, which he repeated in the way which was so characteristic of him to do. He had to read Ida B. Wells and W.E.B. DuBois on his own. He had followed Dr. and Mrs. Coretta Scott King in the papers. Mr. Ross wasn't one-hundred percent certain how to pronounce DuBois, whether to say W-E-B Do-Boys or Web Do-Boyce. He wasn't sure about Ma-Dom or Ma-Dam Cure-ee either. They didn't offer languages at

L.H.S., except three years of German. He knew to pronounce Ger-bells with a soft G.

***

April weather in Antarctica was anybody's guess. Earl the Pearl was the world's last climate-change denier and apocalyptically proud of this fact. Jim was certain that Earl's studied ignorance had everything to do with his vested interest in golf courses and filthy rich friends in oil and gas. Jim worked every angle to deny Earl opportunity to bloviate on such subjects. Few things mildly annoyed Jim as often as Earl or gibberish, but Earl's gibberish could incense him. Some just feel the need to barge up and down a north-south river in Egypt, Jim said. Jim Murry saw himself as a face-the-facts kind of guy, while he saw the Pearl as a walking/talking result of years of natural irritation, or, Jim conceded, maybe Earl was nothing more threatening than a Southbound Zax.

The weather (as opposed to the climate), had for a time turned relatively balmy. The team had a rare day off (a euphemism for a day very much full of work but not involving a game) before beginning a bicoastal road trip early the next morning. The off-day, and the welcome nearly summer weather, filled the diamond with optimism and levity. One guy who played quarterback at the state's flagship university tossed a football to another guy who played wide-out at its struggling land-grant. Jeff put an end to this little shop of horrors. His safety-first interventions were the day's only negativity.

The Phenom arrived early at the park with his 1-win and 1-loss record in tow. He seemed unburdened somehow. His every move was lighter, easier, in retrospect, freer. There he was consulting with the physical therapists; there he was stretching his over-stretched hamstrings. A broad smile crossed his face when Sato, showing off his remarkable prowess, hit a ball far and high into the leftfield pool. Jeff nixed that too.

The next anyone would remember seeing him, The Little Prince was jogging around the stadium, not on the warning track the way most do, but on the concourse below the press box and glass-enclosed suites. He headed toward the Fountain Level, kids play area, and Wall of Fame & Statuary, then back around to the gift store, customer service, and first aid station. He ran past The Serious Sausage Shop and World's Largest Dip-'N-Drip Ice Cream Emporium. Loop after loop, churning the cream and sugar, a smile across tear-etched cheek veins and forehead valleys. Even Hal Newhouser looked down with approval as the Little Prince whistled past the statuary. Inner volcanic heat achieved equilibrium with the day's rising temps and a typically frozen bronze visage melted like Italian ice in a summer Chicago sun. Loop after loop.

***

The team's most recent losing pitcher tried to maintain balance and steady his gait during each of a mounting number of circumnavigations. Despite efforts at self-regulation, Lap 5 started bloody-minded and progressed to homicidal. Newhouser, a plaque read, pitched the triple crown in 1945, which is to say, Prince Hal led the league in wins, strikeouts, and ERA in the year of our lord, one-thousand and forty-five. The Little Prince frowned and tensed. Newhouser hadn't liberated Dachau. He wasn't KIA on Okinawa. He didn't photograph a G.I. there cradling a babe for the world to behold. Prince Hal did not discern a response to Patton, Tito, or Stalin. He did not stop Truman before give 'em hell Harry could dial-up Superfortresses by the hundreds to incinerate Imperial Japan *and all who happened to live there.* Hal Newhouser threw balls and strikes and fouls, when any real hero might have thrown himself over that little boy.

***

The jogger's path was suddenly blocked by a man using a wheelchair and what appeared to be a mother and her daughter.

Whoa, I'm sorry. I didn't see you.

We're sorry. We didn't see *you*. When we did…I'm darn slow with this equipment.

No worries. No worries.

No, it's entirely… Hey, aren't you….

It's him, it's him!

No, I'm not anything.

I know who you are.

You know.

I know who you are.

Are you sure.

Oui.

Truly.

Oui.

D'accord.

It's him!

Enchanté.

You're funny.

Don't be confused. I throw right-handed, in case it makes a difference to you.

I work here, too.

My daughter means that she *volunteers*. She gathers balls fouled off down the left-field line.

My name is Lucy. Just Lucy.

We're the Higgins', actually: Lucy, Maria, and I'm Dan. We're here on a tour because of Lucy. They let us run free. Again, sorry to be in your way. You were training.

I was thinking. And running.

I know all about you.

You said.

I have researched your story.

You have.

Honey, we should let this young man continue his training.

No, it's okay. I was done. I mean, I am done. And, besides, I want to hear what …Lucy, right….what Lucy has discovered.

Oh, we've heard it and it's nothing about which to speak.

It is something, mother. I believe that it is.

I'll sign your hat if you tell me.

I seek not autographs. I will tell you what I know sans bounty.

Do tell.

I found a record of your birth: Montgomery County, Ohio.

Yes.

I found a record of your death, too: Riley County, Kansas.

I'm sorry, sir. We explained, and, of course, she knows.

He's someone with the same name as you. I thought that was so weird. Want to know what's even more astonishing. He was a baseball player, like you.

Word.

My word is my bond. And do you know how I discovered all of this. Well, I will tell you. I called his father, who is still alive. I called him and we talked. He told me all sorts of things about his son, how he was opposed to The Wall, how he once traveled to deepest, darkest Peru, how he was reckless. We talked, he and I, and he said he was glad to have done so. He didn't know me but said he trusted that I was on the side of the angels. He told me that someone named Victor Roother had said the same to *him* once, and that he felt transported to another planet when he said it, if only for a second.

This man must have asked what motivated your call.

Why, you're famous. He and I first connected online. Seeing where I lived, he assumed he knew why I was in touch. He said that he had been thinking of you too.

***

Perfection is a fixed mindset mythology and we should celebrate its demise. Bring on the messiness of indeterminate outcomes and long and winding roads. Last night's game will forever define what baseball means to this observer, this student, this fan. Folks, it's a game meant for pleasure and amusement, nothing more, nothing less.

***

After predicting the Sox's victory last night—and I would have been glad to have been wrong—let me imbibe another spoonful of the breakfast of champions I'm enjoying and predict a winning seasons' first road trip. The Mariners, Red Sox, and Orioles pose real challenge, but Our Boys are in fine form and raring to take their show on the road. Hats off especially to Dave Shoal, the architect of a rejuvenated veteran squad. In fact, dear reader, I will go you one better: Shoal's team is ready—it has the right ingredients—to make a semi-splashy post-season appearance. Mark my words: we will play the Yankees, Rays, or A's, possibly the Rangers, in game one of a losing divisional series.

Jim read the *Free Press* and the *News* religiously, and thought the former was a misnomer and latter was a stretch.

EIGHT

Default programming for Mozart® was Mozart. If Jeff turned the system on but failed to select one of eight-hundred available satellite channels, or if he wasn't engaged in one or more incoming or outgoing calls, *Don Giovanni* or *The Barber of Seville* spritzed the passenger cabin. Varying with who was alongside, wills to live could be dampened. If, however, Jeff was preoccupied by his stint with the Florida Fire Frogs, a passenger might toggle, and, if otherwise unable to discern a direct path to Curtis James Jackson III, might settle on alternative Mozart selections, *The Requiem* in D minor for example. Satisfied there was nothing more to be done, a passenger might sink into the sonorous environment and accept immersion in its somber genius. The never laconic Jeff Millsaps wouldn't notice or mind if he did. As was to be expected with a minor league manager of such promise, Jeff was soon to be promoted to Rome, USA.

***

Before The Villages, about which it would be easy to make more than was there to make, the Little Prince's life flowed through multiple locations (states, cities, sports franchises), multiple family units (blood, blended, thermonuclear), and varying positions in the prevailing system of stratification (upstairs, downstairs, BFE, GED). As with many things, weaknesses were strengths and vice versa. His life had given him the ability to see many sides of things, especially the undersides. It had also given him access to those undersides, which were enriching, endangering, and reason itself to partake of their worst elements. Would naïveté be preferable if, in exchange, one earned peace of mind. Since the garden, people have stood leery before apples, while in advanced industrial society, garden row apartments are accented with Mylar plastic Alar trees.

His mind raced. The Little Prince had only one mind and had never been in another, but he felt that his must be unnatural or exactly what it was made to be. After so many leaps from one universe of discourse to another, he asked himself: was he exhausted by the loneliness that always accompanied him during the pursuit. Palmer, McGregor, Tiant: their jerseys protected his skin but left him cold. Sports journalists had generally missed this point, as he discovered from perusing contraband.

Beyond their journalism, which could be fun, lay literature. To the Little Prince's way of thinking, literature was more important than anything he knew. The Little Prince tried in vain to offer an original definition. He said for a time that literature was death-defying acts of writing against every possible grain and sinew. He felt confirmed in this view when he discovered that Sartre ranked literature ahead of philosophy and declined the Nobel Prize because of it. History was sacred to him as well. History kept the Little Prince pinned down. It located him in time and space, both of which were infinite as far as he knew.

This is why the Little Prince ingested literature and history, his religion and grounding, and this is why he rarely meshed easily with dugout teammates. Even if he entertained them, pandered to their wants and tastes, even if he wowed them with incredible tricks, such as his wellspring of strikes; would they ever understand him, they in their world, he in his. Would he ever connect. The Little Prince was not un-self-critical. He crashed now and again. He wasn't all that good at flying solo. In the aftermath of a crash, he might wander searchingly though blazing desert moonlight or convalesce in some hospital. At such times, the Little

Prince watched as others passed overhead. He usually couldn't tell if they were even looking for him. He watched as they passed in and out his hospital room. Sometimes they would check his temperature, but few inquired beyond the raw data.

These feelings and experiences did not explain why the Little Prince played baseball. Why would a precocious boy who knew he was human waste what was left of his time on baseball. Even the Hall of Famer, Al Kaline, regretted not becoming at least a medical doctor. The Little Prince had been groomed, it was true, but he had options. The Little Prince qua baseball player felt that he must appear queer, or would, if anyone knew what was inside his uniform. While he acknowledged that the two things didn't go together—that he and baseball were a contradiction—the Little Prince embraced this earthly project, and, as best he could, sought to elevate it within reason. In the face of what felt unavoidable—the given, the here and now, the sound and the fury—the Little Prince figured he would either pitch a most perfect perfect-game or he would just as well die trying.

People are disappointing.

The notion occurred to him all too often and saddened him every time it did. He could carve his body into the surface of Mars, but no one really cared. No one said, we can, and we shall, repair this skin. He would hear faint queries: Are you all right. I hope you are all right. I'm not there, but I hope you are.

The Little Prince sometimes thought to use a lantern in broad daylight in search of honest men. When at his most and least philosophical, he imagined that we were celestial bondsman: living, partly living, or dead. We have no choice, the Little Prince believed, but orbit our star until it implodes. We're bound to this speck until rock melts and reforms anew. Geological determinism, he called it. Then, and only then, our atoms may be cast out of this and into another universe or two. Practically speaking, we're here to stay in one form or the other. We're grounded. We're infield dirt, he would say.

***

Fan Favorite, LLC, kept a bulletin board with lists of what had been fished out of their fountains over the years. Richard, Fan Favorite's number two, conducted a central tendency analysis that identified, not unexpectedly, children's dolls as the item-list mode. Children's dolls just loved to play in the fountains' waterfalls and were often as not the primary source of any number of exciting downstream problems. Both Richard and his CEO, Nora May, happened to be in attendance when a life-size buddy doll caused panic in sections 700 and 800 before its dramatic rescue. As he and Nora May both knew, tearful soggy-sized doll incidents were as commonplace as store-bought funerary cuisine. Unmarried Piggies. Cabbage Kids. G.I. Josés. Wonderous Women.

Rings, including especially wedding rings, were top-enders too, as were earrings, nose-rings, ear-studs, nose-studs, and other assorted bling. Items for baby came in third, while items for adult babies (jewel-incrusted cigarette lighters, tiaras, grillz, gold-platted keys to Kevlar-platted Hummers), as a general category, were a close fourth.

Outliers most intrigued Fan Favorite's sleuths. There was the case of the non-descript guitar pick. Seriously, dude, Richard had said right to the man's face. And a lost rabbits' *head*. Nora May still winced. The talisman that left the most vivid impression, and which was depicted graphically in Tony's skilled pencil sketch on Fan Favorite's employee bulletin board wall, was an ocular prosthesis that had shot out of a double leg-amputee's left socket as she reached gamely, and, as it turned out, unwisely, for a distant chance at a desired game souvenir. At least she didn't lose more of herself, Richard would smirk. Nora May echoed in kind: at least she's no longer seeing double.

***

Reflecting on her day, Lucy recalled a Petit Prince tee shirt at Cesar's Used Books. Mrs. Quintin, the proprietor, sold a selection of tees that featured works of literature. The shirt Lucy had noticed was a lovely blue, its front a cartoonish rendering of the eponymous title character and what she recalled as moons and stars and asteroids as background. Maybe her favorite ballplayer would accept a present. Extra-large, maybe double extra-large, Lucy reasoned. She might stroll to the dugout, which wasn't far. The diamond girl might quip: *Say hey little prince, I got something for you.* Lucy saw herself tossing the shirt, but she wasn't sure if he could catch as well as he dished.

***

His kitchen had gone from bad to worse to combustible. Dishes hadn't piled in the sink so much as the sink had become a giant dish (much as Chuck Norris doesn't get wet when he steps into the ocean, the ocean, it is said, gets Chuck Norris). Stove grease refracted light. Warm milk turned into fire-hazard cheese. (Fire might—might—be this problem's most efficient solution, Jeff thought.) Spring had turned unmanageable to unbreathable. Jeff suggested he hire help. Jeff stressed that there was no way on God's Green Earth that the hired help in question would be Jeff. For some reason, vermin were not an issue; mold, mildew, and a micro-organism ecosystem were an issue. Untold tiny amphibious earth creatures inhabited a mysterious black lagoon.

A new century Gregor Samsa lived in a rambling wreck of a place, but for its largest living inhabitant, it was the rug to his bug. A crummy apartment in a crummy urban apartment complex in a middling city was a post-Villages sanctuary, a new lease on life. Above all, it was the means and measure of his independence. Thanks to Mrs. S., a young man not even eighteen lived unfettered by petty authority and hurtful slings and arrows. Enthralled by the possibility of higher purposes, Billy Budd set down soon after moving in and drafted an Apartment Constitution. Its natural law framework would guide visitor behavior and set the boundaries for future democratic deliberation. The founding notes and papers have been lost to history, but their secular humanism is best captured in an oft-repeated snippet from The Glorious Preamble: *Don't be a Dick*.

***

He needed to pack. The team took care of most of what needed doing. His uniforms, cleats, gloves—these would be packed and shipped by clubhouse staff. But each player was expected to bring their own street clothes and toiletries for a ten-day out-of-town trip, which was no problem for a collection of millionaires, expert travelers who, thanks in part to Jim, were reasonably style conscious. Sitting in his one-bedroom, one-bath mansion, the Little Prince wondered if he had anything in which to store clothes and deodorant, let alone whether he had clothes and deodorant to store.

No one had asked him if he needed help. Mrs. S. had said little last night. Jeff regaled him with stories from the minor leagues during the ride home today, out of nervousness or as a way of keeping things light, Jeff's method of staying close. What would Jim think if the Little Prince showed up at the charter terminal wearing his best tan khakis and a holey red sweater from the Salvation Army. What if his luggage were a duffle bag and backpack, the former army issued, the latter with one working shoulder harness. Would Jim be glad just to see him or look at him like a disappointed dad. In spite of his recent achievements, the Little Prince knew that he was rags, the riches surrounding him out of reach. His stomach tightened.

***

Whenever things looked bleak, it helped to connect with his Droogs, who, as Droogs are wont to do, appreciated pieces of him that others didn't, couldn't, or wouldn't. Those still in-residence at the Villages were not allowed contact with the outside world sans prior permission and staff supervision. But he had alternative mates in his imaginary rolodex, old friends he met through youth baseball leagues, high schools, writer groups, youth ministries, and an especially active Asian-American student rights group. These relationships pre- and post-dated stints in two short-term locked ward facilities, a blow-up involving Florida law enforcement, and kind invitation to The Villages. Mrs. S.'s interference in the last was, as far as he knew, non-existent, and neither she nor he were any longer curious as to her thinking. Like others, the Little Prince knew people from the places where he had lived and traveled. Time and space were no barrier to his many virtual friendships. The problem was that they were virtual.

No one appeared immediately available this evening. Had he scalded himself in boiling water, he would have had to drive his burned flesh to the E.R. himself. Were he flush with pizza and beer, he would have had to consume them solo. If the son of god had showed up at his door and wanted to meet his friends—really get to know them, perhaps absolve their sins—the son of god would have to cool his sacred heels until maybe after ten o'clock or so, but probably for longer. That's what came back from casting the net worldwide: not a single fish and nothing—not even baseball—on TV.

Jim and Jeff had been pushing the *Scouting Report*. There it sat. This tome was different than the type of scouting reports that are prepared on prospects. He had never seen his prospect scouting report, and, given Mrs. S.'s pivotal role in his situation, he doubted there even was one.

Scouting was partly art but mostly science, even though it hadn't always been that way. When Hal Newhouser signed as an eighteen-year-old, a scout might have written a few sentences: Harold is a six feet two-inch left-handed pitcher who bats from the left side. He is a sturdy 180 pounds. Good attitude. Hometown kid. Should get along fine with Greenberg. Newhouser: *recommended.*

The Little Prince knew that it was unfair to cast aspersions against Prince Hal and his Hallmark card family. Hal had a heart-valve problem. As much as it would have made his life immeasurably easier, the military refused Hal Newhouser's request to die on a beach, in a jungle, parceled out in pieces on a road traversing a faraway formally bucolic countryside. Hal Newhouser had no choice. It wasn't his fault he was a hero.

The scouting reports on Mariners, Red Sox, and Orioles hitters were a different story. Thanks to Sabermetrics and its offspring, for each hitter there was recorded one-hundred separate cells of information and summary recommendations. Rob Winston, the Mariner second baseman, hits twenty-three percent of pitches thrown but forty-percent of those which dared cross the inside half of the plate. He is from Wichita Falls and attended Rice University, where he played on a College Worlds Series Runner-Up and set a Series record for participation in successful double-plays. Winston is a jazz pianist and enjoys fishing and hunting. He is single but is in a committed relationship. Rob votes a straight Republican ticket because his father did, and he couldn't hit a curve ball if it were hand-delivered from the mound by Oompa Loompa and placed carefully on a T-ball stand. Recommendation: every time Rob Winston dares ask for more, feed him a liberal diet of Everlasting Gobstoppers on the outer half of the plate.

***

Humor had been a big part of his life. The Little Prince owned a coffee table collection of *New Yorker* cartoons and he consumed a lot of stand-up, from Louis C.K. (ambivalence) to Marc Maron (admiration) to Dave Chappelle (pledge of fealty). *The Onion* made his twitter feed cry. He knew that the depressed, young men especially, often identified with this genre. He was no different. He couldn't tell a joke to save his soul, but he liked to laugh and to be tickled. He loved to feel anything, unfortunately.

It was at this point that he decided to eat a dozen spoonful of smooth peanut butter that he kept in his bedroom and snort a few lines of (unbeknownst to himself) fentanyl-laced heroin that he had stored in the kitchen. The fat in the peanut butter made its consumption immensely pleasurable, each dollop a delight, especially when mixed with still-drinkable milk from the lit 'fridge.

Now, while he was at the kitchen counter and had a knife in his hand, it was time to trim straws and prepare lines. The alarm was set for four o'clock. He needed eight hours of sleep and respite from his overactive mind. He would not miss the plane or cause it to depart late. Mrs. S. was due at five o'clock and he would not disappoint her, unless, that is, the fentanyl-laced heroin he was inhaling caused his breathing to stop, then his brain activity, and then his beating heart. If this were to happen, then the Little Prince would be dead.

***

Dr. Sweetwater made his way upstairs, slowly and with extra care. He was still healing. He had warmed a cup of milk and said eureka upon discovering anise cookies in a high cupboard. He lapped milk and nibbled cookies while downstairs, not steady enough to manage ascent with liquid hands on an empty stomach. Mary had insisted he send her an e-mail before he turned in. She worried. The stress of his illness would have been enough, but the situation with Margie Stefanski weighed on her dad. Mary still had a good bit of her own work in need of her attention:

reports, letters, review of an unusual number of hospitalized patients. She was even working on a co-authored paper for publication. Dr. Mary now stocked her SUV as an emergency vehicle and kept her phone near for any circumstance. Dr. Mary Sweetwater quietly slipped back downstairs.

***

When Jeff couldn't sleep, no one could sleep. Not content to have every television blaring in common areas, not content to pace in his study, not adverse to solo billiards in the game room or late-night dips in his brightly lit, echo-chamber indoor pool, Jeff was calmed, was truly calmed, only by the intimate fellowship of his beloved family, *his girls*, as he called them. Tina Marie, the youngest, was the first to concede defeat.

Dad, when are you going to bed.

Sorry, honey. Go back to sleep. We have a big road trip tomorrow. Daddy will be gone for over a week, you know.

Jeff, honey, we wish you were gone now.

Oh, are you up too.

Jeff, honey, we're all up. Bless your heart, you have every TV on in the house.

I'm having a hard time. I am worried.

What are you worried about. The Mariners aren't that good this year, are they.

No, it's not that. It's not even baseball.

Is it Jim. Are you worried about how he's handling the hubbub.

Yes, I am worried about Jim, but I am much more worried about our Phenom. Jeannie, do you know how much pressure he's under. I don't think he's up to it. There are a lot people who don't know his situation. A lot people do not know it, yet.

Like what, dear.

Oh, Jeannie. You know I would tell you, but it's a workplace thing. I know it's hard to imagine sometimes, but these kids are employees. They have rights under the law.

If you don't want to tell me, that's fine. I didn't really want to ask, tell you the truth.

Why do you say that.

I don't know. I am tired. We have to get up early to see you off. I have to take care of the kids again for over a week on my own, and I do have a job, too, you know.

I know, darling. It's hard on all of us. But there is some compensation, you'd have to admit. I mean, we live well.

It depends on what you mean by well, Jeff. You're stressed or gone or stressed *and* gone. We have a pool but what's that going to matter when you have a stroke one night and we fish you out in the morning. And don't get me started on what you miss in the girls' lives. You know the story. We've been over that a thousand times.

Jeff's nerves were not being calmed by Jeannie and their conversation, and all the while she was talking, Jeff couldn't think of much else than the sleep he wasn't getting and the boy he wasn't helping. Jeff had grave concern for his young pitcher, who was living in a dump across town and probably didn't have a suitcase to pack for the trip.

***

Dave had a neat stack of newspapers on his desk at home. He liked to stay abreast of national trends. He felt this alone justified a modest household staff who would keep things just-so. Dave poured himself a single-malt scotch on the rocks from a bottle he purchased in Scotland and re-read a few local columns. His principal concern, however, was the wire services and their reports from the senior circuit. It was not out of the question, Dave thought, that he could be a viable candidate for commissioner. That was part of the reason why he read as much as he could. But he would probably also need as much success with his team as, say, a Bud Selig had had with his. The veteran squad poised for its first road trip—the squad Dave had painstakingly assembled—might be enough to check that box, especially if Mrs. S.'s wild card pitcher could win a few games over the course of the season in addition to what Dave had already penciled in.

It occurred to Dave in this moment that he had a lot riding on Millsaps. It wasn't too late. He decided to give Jeff a call, to let him know what this trip meant to the team.

***

Jim's office had an *objet d'art* that was unlike the others. He had commissioned several, including an oil painting depicting Jim Northup's game six grand slam. The detail of Northup's face drew many offers. Another portrait, this one in ink, depicted Armando Gallaraga standing in repose on the mound, his outline brilliant against a withering sun. Jim said he wouldn't part with this sketch if it meant he had to survive during his later years eating cat food. He felt similarly about an oil of Chet Lemon's reluctant walk-off home run curtain call. The smile and wave of his cap was caught perfectly, thought Jim, who had been there as a kid, a living witness to the scene depicted. Jim recalled the Jays' reliever standing in the aftermath, bowed in meditation, prayer, or sports psychology visualization. The stadium *shook*. Among Jim's table-size sculptures were one each in pewter of Mickey Lolich and Milt Wilcox, and a Remington-style obstructed view of the beloved old stadium before all the shaking took it down.

Standing apart from the semi-nice stuff was Jim's Jack Nicklaus Desk Phone, a hunk of white plastic that he bought forty-five years prior and since maintained against all reason. It was one of the first popularly for sale that featured speed-dial function. Scooter found it appalling and in this one opinion was not alone. Jim claimed that it worked just fine but he knew he had had it repaired three times. We make so much junk, Jim said, let's honor something which somehow evaded planned obsolescence. Jim was reminiscing again about his long-deceased stepfather, with whom he watched an inordinate amount of golf, when the Golden Bear drove squarely into his daydream.

It's Jim. _____

Hey, Jim. Martin here. I wonder if I could set up an exclusive interview with your newest starter.

Martin, first, do me a favor and go through Scooter on this. Second, know that Dave has decided that we won't be doing interviews, so don't hold your breath.

What do you mean, no interviews.

It's our policy. You were at the press conference.

I do not understand.

We're not doing advertising around him, either. You haven't seen any commercials or heard any radio spots. Have we taken out a page in your paper. No.

But I'm talking about something dignified, Jim. Roger Angell. Frank DeFord.

Grantland Rice, I know.

Jim, I'm serious. This is important. I think Lester and I might do a book together.

I think you and Lester are getting ahead of yourselves.

It was historic what he did. I don't care what you say or how you aim to play it down, it was historic. He's a hero, too, I'm guessing. But I need to talk with that kid to know with certainty. His second outing wasn't bad either, if you ask me. If he would have thrown more breaking balls or at least an effective change-up, he might have….

Could'ves and should'ves, Martin. And now I'm starting to take this personally.

SAY HEY LITTLE PRINCE

***

Reggie Ross lived with his girlfriend in a Cape Cod starter on Cleveland Avenue. By the time he wobbled in after the game, once he had dropped Grandpa off at his place six blocks away, Felicia was already in bed. Unlike most people, and unlike his namesake particularly, Reggie took the kid's loss hard. He was miffed like most people weren't when Murry had the nerve to pull a pitcher with a no-hitter. What the heck was that. C'mon Gramps, he has a no-no going and he's being sent to the showers. It's not right. Reggie shook his head and loudly proclaimed the injustice, the wrong, the grave mistake. It's not right. It's not right, not right at all. No sir. No sir. Not good. Not right.

Picking gently through the medicine chest for some plop-plop-fizz-fizz, it occurred to Reggie that he felt awfully passionate about baseball. It was merely a game, Grampa chided him, but why would Reggie put any stock in what someone has to say who spent his whole life following the team like he was a silent owner. It mattered, Reggie understood, that he and Grampa had met the pitcher in person. What a cool thing that was. He felt a bond unlike how he might have otherwise felt. Reggie recalled his moist brown eyes, intuitive graciousness, and the obvious distress he worked to mask. He seemed both old and young, caught between the on-ramp and the curving highway. Reggie said the last to himself aloud, but softly. He sure didn't want to disturb Felicia.

***

When the Bronze Man knocked at thirty minutes past ten o'clock post meridiem, Jim was especially deep in English Oval bliss. Consequently, he startled noticeably.

Hey boss, sorry to bother.

Harold, geez, you startled me. What are you doing. It's late.

I had a few things I needed for the trip tomorrow and you know I live close.

Yeah.

I saw you in here and thought maybe we could talk a minute.

Sure, of course. May I get you something.

You got a bottle of water.

I do. Do you want artisan spring water, imported water from France, or flavored water with…let's see…three choices: blackberry, strawberry, or grape.

Just water, skip. Thanks.

Artisan spring water, it is. I shall partake of some France.

Listen, this season has started with a bang, hasn't it.

It has, Harold. The amount of scrutiny and attention, I wouldn't have predicted that. But you guys are handling it well. We're all grateful for that.

Most of us veterans are. How are you doing, Jim.

I'm the old sea-dog, Harold. I was *retired* from the game before you were born.

But you're just human like the rest of us. My pops, he's a minister, you recall. He taught me to see the world from the point of view of the not-born and the people who've been called, you know what I mean.

Here's a coaster. That table is an antique.

He taught me to keep the daily stuff in perspective, you know.

Sure. I know you're a leader among leaders.

I'm not talking about baseball, Skip.

Well, sure. I know you're not.

Can I tell you a story. My Pops used to tell his congregation this story. Got to remember, my people are all from Houston. 'Stros fans, all of them. Pop would get them to think about J. R. Richard. How he was on top of the world and then he has that stroke, nearly dies from a fool blood clot in his throat. Course it was so disappointing, how his career was cut-off. But pop reminds them that ole James Rodney found a new vocation, a new voice, becomes a minister himself.

I met him once.

Me, too, boss. A lot more than once. That man inspired me in sport. I might not be a ballplayer were it not for The Right Reverend, Mr. J. R. Richard.

I'm not sure I have discerned the point of your story, Harold. It's late.

Life is bigger than baseball, or sport. I'm worried about you, Jim. I feel like a blood clot is coming for you, man. I have a feel for these things. I might have never told you, but that's how I won that medal. I could feel when the gun was about to go off. I was always the first out of them blocks, Jim. Watch the film. Always the first, man.

***

Earl was in Pearl mode as he strove through SeaTac. To the supreme irritation of his sister, he arrived in Seattle a day ahead of the team. She asked him to stay because she might need his help, but he brushed her request aside with an old wives' tale about a brewing coffee bean business deal. Earl, I am not going to ask twice. And she didn't.

Earl was basking in generic glory at a coffee shop franchise location that he imagined replicating throughout rural America, destroying the local café in the same way that ole Sam Walton destroyed small town grocery stores. His special line lit up.

Yes.

Earl.

Yes.

It's Dr. Sweetwater.

Dr. Sweetwater.

Yes, your sister's friend.

Oh, sure. How are you.

Terrible. But listen. Margie needs to get to Rochester today, if this is at all possible. She needs immediate emergency medical attention, do you understand, Earl.

What are you talking about.

I'm sorry to tell you, and by rights I shouldn't, but your sister has a tumor and it needs to be looked at immediately. There's no time to waste.

Well, I....

No one knows about it. You know how she can be. She's not acting on my recommendation the way she needs to. That's why I'm calling you.

I'm in Seattle. We have a three-game series here starting tomorrow.

What's more important, Earl. I ask you that. What's more important.

Listen, Sam, I know what's important. Why isn't Margie doing what you suggested. That's the part that doesn't make sense.

She's distracted by that kid. She wants to protect the kid.

What kid are we talking about, Sam.

***

Jim stretched himself along his leather bed and pulled a hand-knitted afghan over him, a relic from his most recent spouse that he kept underneath the sofa. It was late. The fountains were silent. If it was clear as Jim thought, the stars would light the ponds' still surfaces and a gibbous moon would perform ritual Aztec surgery. Jim's mind pictured the sacrifice without looking away. He recalled that men in his youth thought it a hoot to toss newborn human beings across living rooms. They would sit semi-circular and shovel-passed stardust from love seat to chair to couch, high over gods' footstools.

Stardust.

NINE

Mrs. S. sat on her bed. She wasn't sure if she was crying uncontrollably because she was by herself, or if she was by herself because she intuited desperate need for space to be herself completely, something a woman in her position was rarely, perhaps never, allowed to be. It was before noon. She had been home more than an hour. She couldn't really keep track of time. Her Cartier diamond watch was of no help to her at all. Mrs. S. felt that her body was in rebellion against the thin veneer of normalcy that smothers lives. The lump on the back of her neck had grown since earlier that morning, given a new lease, she supposed, by the unspeakable death of her dear Petit Prince.

Mrs. S. closed her eyes and moaned and growled. Blue and red lights still bathed the insides of her eyelids. A police officer—Officer Felix—had confirmed what she knew. She wondered, given her presence of mind to request discretion, if she really loved him as deeply as she thought she did. Margaret Stefanski's mind raced in five directions at once, but every few seconds she returned to the wrenching realization that her prince, who she had named and loved, was suddenly, shockingly, horribly and forever gone. This thought was unbearable. She knew it was not survivable; she would not survive.

***

Jeff had been the second civilian at the scene. His black SUV screamed to a stop in a street filled with emergency vehicles and business-like patrolmen faces. He felt an Ole Miss surge of adrenaline as he raced past Mrs. S. and didn't stop running until a detective prevented him from reaching for the door. No, he said. Please god, no. The detective looked at him blankly. Please, no. Please, god, no. A phrase often repeated, with the word tragedy interjected. It's an incomprehensible tragedy, Jeff said to no one. A staggering tragedy. Please god, no. Please god, no. It's a mind-boggling tragedy. Through world-shattering pain, a time-altering fog, Jeff couldn't stop saying again and again and again; no, please god; no, please god; no, please god, no, please god, no.

***

Mary, it's your father.

What is it, dad.

I know it's unexpected, and early too, but could you come with me. Margie just called. She told me that that young man who pitched so well, that he's died in his sleep. I need to help her, Mary. I...

Oh, dad.

I need to see Margie, to help her.

Dad, you're crying.

Yes, I am crying. Damn straight I am crying. Men cry, you know. I damn sure cry. I cry every day, I'll have you know, about every day since your mother's been gone.

Dad, I'm almost in the car.

***

Jim was awakened by Lester, who was, to Jim's astonishment, standing directly over him.

Lester. Jesus. What in blazes.

Jim, I am sorry.

Lester. You scared the blazes out of me. What are you doing in my office at..., what the heck time is.

Jim, I let myself in the back way. I thought you might be here.

What is happening, Lester. Can you answer me that.

Jim, I have tragic news. I was up early because Bud wanted me to tag along on this road trip, and, you know, old habits die hard. I was listening to the police scanner, Jim. I heard the news.

What news, Lester. What are you talking about.

Jim, I hate to be the one to tell you this. It's not my forte.

Jesus, Lester.

Jim, your kid, Maxwell, he's dead. He died, Jim. Died in his sleep, it appears.

What. What are you saying. What did you say to me.

It's Max, Jim. He died at his apartment last night. Mrs. Stefanski found him. She was giving him a ride this morning. He didn't answer her texts and calls. She had a key, I guess. Anyhow, he died in his sleep, Jim. Jeff called me. I'm so sorry, Jim. I truly am.

***

Samuel Kenneth Robertson let slip through his sure hands the Morir Soñando he was preparing as breakfast. His drink met the kitchen floor and reprised Alamogordo. Sammy froze and did nothing but continue to listen to the radio. Died in his sleep, he thought. He knew what that probably meant. Maybe the kid had an enlarged heart, maybe a blood clot. But chances were, something bad. Sammy's spouse sputtered hurriedly into the room. He held up his hand in the universal sign for: don't move.

***

Earl, I'm not talking on the phone.

Listen, Margie, you need to take care of yourself. I'll have Walker help you.

Earl, you will do no such thing. Walker works for me, not you. And I make decisions about me, not my younger brother. Is that clear. Now, goodbye.

Don't hang up, Margie. Don't you hang up. Dr. Sweetwater says it's an emergency.

And don't you think I don't have a few words for Sam Sweetwater. Goodbye.

***

Once he packed Lester off with gratitude for his concern and ritual well-wishes, Jim sat in pulsing shock, not knowing what next to do. How much time had passed, he didn't know. He wasn't one-hundred percent certain of his location. It was his office, but where was his office. He floated to wash his face. What happened. What should he do. Mr. S's books stared blankly and provided cold comfort. He felt nothing for them in this moment. What happened. What should he have done. A moist death-rattle moan. Tears, uncontrollable tears, flow.

At some point, Jim looked at his cell phone and saw a dozen calls from Jeff. He decided to return one of them. Jeff was sobbing as he answered. This caused Jim, embarrassment notwithstanding, to bray a grieving opera. An awkward few moments passed while Jim existed outside of himself. Quietude prevailed. Jeff talked. Jim sat.

It's so awful, Jim. I had a premonition. I still can't believe it. I got over there as fast as I could. Margie was staring into daybreak. I tried to go in, but they wouldn't let me. God, it was awful. We were there for two or three hours, I'm not sure. They hurried because of Margie, I think. Some reporters appeared. The police kept everyone away.

Jim finally found a prose voice. Why didn't you call.

I tried. I think your ringer is off.

What about the team, Jim asked.

I sent word for them to go ahead. I didn't know what to do. Dave had called me right about then, and he and I, I guess, decided that they should go.

Jeff, I want you to go with the team. I want you to manage the team in Seattle.

Jim, I honestly don't know.

I am not asking, I'll telling you. Be on that flight to Seattle.

***

The doctors Sweetwater stood at Margie's pink door. They had been annoyed to pass two television trucks and a police cruiser as they pulled into her grandly sweeping circular drive. Mary thought she might bring a small case she had packed with her. As he stepped from the vehicle, Sam pulled his tweed jacket close and wondered if he had dressed appropriately, his mind not being what it once was. Mrs. S.'s nephew, Walker, drew open the door but stood behind it mostly lest he be photographed or filmed. The foyer resembled the nave at Ely Cathedral; Mary thought her father's Tudor might fit whole within it. They were directed to sit to one side near a fresh bouquet. Mary asked her father if he had ever visited The Biltmore, and to her surprise, he said that he had. The Elder Dr. Sweetwater said as though to no one that he had once walked its garden ponds.

***

Mr. Ross listened to radio news. He didn't own a television. He had calculated the value of a subscription to two national dailies, added how the game played on the radio, and then multiplied by the harm inflicted by too much visual hot air. In sum, Mr. Ross decided years ago that he and television should remain on limited engagement terms. If Reggie wanted to watch a game, they could go to Darrell's. But if it were his druthers, he'd listen at home, let his imagination do some work. For this reason, and for this reason exclusively, Mr. Ross had begrudging respect for Ronald Reagan, who could concoct a baseball game as well as anyone could, he figured.

Mr. Ross thought about his kid brother. How hard it had been to break the news to his parents. And why was it always him who had to break news. Damn. What did he do to deserve such honors. Reggie would be getting ready for college this morning. Today was Mad Anthony Wayne Community College, tomorrow the bus depot. How was Reggie going to take the news. Was there some way of keeping this loss from him, of stringing him along unawares. Mr. Ross didn't want anything bad to happen to Reggie, whose heart was already too soft. Mr. Ross was protective of hearts and minds.

***

Lucy's name came across the school's P.A. system. She was changing in the change-room and this invasion did nothing to lessen her anxiety. Lucy finished pulling up socks and tying shoes before, as instructed, reporting directly to the main office.

***

Dave was calling from the charter. Was there anything Jim wanted to say to the team. Jim sat in silence.

You there, Jim.

Yes.

Did you hear me. Is there anything you want to say to the team before we push back.

Is Jeff there.

Yes, he boarded.

Have you done a headcount.

Yes, only two short.

What.

Two short, so, you know, we're ready.

What do you mean, *two short*.

Well, you and the kid. That's all. I asked Jorge to help me because, you know, Walker is going to stay with Margie.

Dave, I have nothing to say to you or the team. Goodbye.

Jim hung up his cell phone. Before he knew he was doing it, he stood and ripped Jack Nicklaus from the wall and with both hands raised as high as he could, smashed Fat Jack on his freshly polished parquet floor. Jack did not survive. Few would survive.

***

Dave requested a minute of Jeff's time. What did he think was the right thing to do. Jeff spoke from a place beyond normalcy, as though it were just him and Jeff, two humans fixed on a random celestial body. We play the next three games with god-blessed black arm bands, and we stop at home for a service or funeral or what have you on our way back across the country, before Boston. Period. Dave thought about this plan. It seemed to make sense, but what about the insertion of *period*. Jeff looked at him like his wasn't so much a suggestion from two rungs down, but a firm command from the engine room. Dave scanned the veteran faces seated in neat rows behind him. What he saw varied greatly. Sato, you couldn't tell. Robertson, he wasn't sure. Carlson looked mildly concerned, as did Sanchez, but Harold Morris looked as though he were deep in the throes of labor. Jeff, should someone check on Harold Morris. No, Dave.

***

Margie appeared in the foyer and signaled for the physicians to follow her. She led them slowly through a hallway to the library, where they sat in straight-back cloth Queen Annes amid probably a thousand bound books and two globes each the size of Shakespeare's theater. Margaret donned the visage of Elizabeth I, The Faerie Queene.

Let me get straight to the issues we need to discuss. Mary, thank you for being here. I appreciate your presence. At first, I was hesitant. But I am glad you are here.

If you want me to step out....

No, this will go better if you listen to what I say as though I mean it, manifestly, if you follow. You and Sam are the only people I plan to see today and, if I can manage it, tomorrow and for the foreseeable future.

But you must go to Rochester, Margie.

So that provides segue to the first issue we need to settle. What to do about this golf ball growing on my brainstem. Well, I want you both to listen carefully, because I am about to tell you what we're going to do. Nothing. We—you, me, these books—we are going to do nothing. I have asked Walker to cancel the plane to Minnesota, Sam. I know that one is not supposed to make life-and-death decisions under duress, but I am not one. I am me. I am not going to Minnesota, not today or tomorrow or ever, as far as I am concerned. If Earl or you want to cart my lifeless remains there after I'm dead, then there's nothing I can do about that. Besides, I am damn sure that I won't mind the cold.

Margie.

Don't Margie, me, Sam Sweetwater. Issue two. You had no business sharing my personal medical information with anyone, not even the lovely Dr. Sweetwater here.

Mrs. Stefanski, I agree, and I am sorry about that.

Dear, it's best to be seen right now.

I consider it a personal matter and I will agree to put it behind us if you agree to stop talking to me about the Mayo Clinic. Understood. Which brings me to the third issue. Sam, Mary, I have lost my only child. Do you understand. I'm still not able....

Margie, are you okay.

Heavens no, I'm not okay. You surprise me, Sam. Goodness gracious. A doctor should know, I would think, that it is *not* okay. That it is *never* going to be okay.

He means well, Mrs. S.

And, Mary, for the love of god, I've known you since you were a baby and I know that your father bloody well means well. Listen. Listen to me. I want to share a story. There's not much time. Alek and I never had kids. You know that. You may not know, however, that Alek had a vision. A real vision. He used to talk with rabbis about it.

Rabbis.

Yes, Alek loved to talk with rabbis. A temple should fall in, he used to say.

Was Alek Jewish.

He wouldn't put it that way. His family in Poland were Jewish. Mine, as you know, are Roman Catholic. But neither Alek nor I cared for organized religion; we weren't keen on disorganized religion either. Still, Alek lived for the sacred. His scars notwithstanding, my husband was the most devout man I ever knew. He had a vision. Did I say that.

Yes, Margie.

He felt that his miraculous financial success—and it was, you know— would empower him to make a difference in the world. But he feared that before he could realize his destiny, he would die and his heirs—me, he said, and a surprising young man from another world—would achieve greatness after he was gone. Alek told me the day of his last stroke that he was certain of this and that it would involve the team.

That's an extraordinary story, Mrs. S.

It's all true. All the essential elements are true. I knew upon meeting him that he was meant to fulfill Alek's vision. I can't tell you the things he said. It wasn't that his words cut through darkness; darkness lit his words.

Are you able to share what he said.

Do either of you understand what I just said. Darkness lit his words.

We're listening, Mrs. Stefanski.

He would speak in a strange language. I could understand only bits, a phrase here and there. He said that it is only because of our eyes that we live on *une planète bleue*, making our eyes—our multicolored eyes, you see—the only eyes that count.

Our eyes are the only eyes that count.

He said we are *une affaire littéraire*, and he attempted to live this curious precept in hope, I believe, of making it real. Of course, it's impossible. Who reads. Who lives.

Was he suicidal, Margie.

Much of this, honestly, confounds me.

Was there a note.

He said that he was certain—he insisted—that there were no material changes when we die, only *les histoires de coeur*. When the subject of mortality arose—as I would say it did on occasion, more than I realized at the time—he might twist and look askance. I recall his talking about baseball whenever he was especially pensive. Pitchers should pitch *strikes*. He was emphatic. Strikes. It made good baseball sense.

I think you know that he didn't care for the game of baseball—strictly speaking, you understand, the *game* of baseball—any more than I do. But others cared. Jim and Jeff cared. He played along to learn what was true and right. What else is there to do.

I assumed that he was addicted to baseball.

Hardly. He told me that he once swam in the lit fountain pools. He fished out a rusted Congo Free State Franc near what they call Belgium.

What happened to him, Mrs. Stefanski.

Sam, do you know what any of this means. They said it was an accident, a garden variety accident. Did my precocious boy strike a bargain for poison fruit.

We understand.

Listen, I must tell you this, it's the only way to honor him. You are friends and you are doctors, but I am reasonably certain that you do not—do *not*—*understand*. Oh dear, the pain. The loss, you know, is rending. When Alek died, his graveyard crackled beneath my winter boots. It grew softer as I put distance between me and him, but the snowpack spoke to me. Now, honestly, I hear Larsen Shelf crashing into the Southern Ocean. It's deafening beyond recognition. I'm lost, Sam. Mary, dear, I'm feeling quite dizzy. Do you think my tumor has matured. Do you think it's ready to be on its own.

***

Akihiko looked through Dave Shoal, who scanned the aircraft as though he were counting students on a train to the zoo. Akihiko recalled such trips. Ueno Station was a revelation to the young Akihiko. When they returned there again and again to visit the many museums, Akihiko always remembered to be grateful for the Ueno Station, which he did not see as a passive medium through which one passed to gain knowledge on the outside, but as itself a source of knowledge, knowledge for and from and about the inside. Its high glass ceiling was a metaphor, Akihiko imagined, for the world outside of human knowing. We could know what we could think and feel, but that left almost everything beyond our grasp. He also reflected on the many train lines and their different intersecting colors. The colors did not blur but remained distinct. They shared much, yet retained independent identities, each for and against the other, perhaps. The buses were beautiful, too. The monorail at Ueno Zoo was a lesson. Akihiko was enamored with all things inexplicable; he was, he knew, raised after the end of the world. Akihiko said a favorite prayer: *the ineffable is sticky rice and steamed vegetables.*

***

Lucy, it's your father.

Dad, is something the matter.

Yes, but your mother and I are okay. Don't jump to conclusions.

Okay, are you sure.

Yes, dear.

But what is it. Is it Nana or Grandpa John.

No, dear. I hate to tell you this, but I worried that you'd hear from someone at school. The thing is, sweetheart, that young man, the Little Prince…he has….

Oh my god. Oh my god, no. Oh my god, no.

Dear. Dear. Lucy, sweetheart. Listen to me. Your mother can take off from work, if you want. She's able to come get you. Gather your things. Why don't you come home.

***

Sammy sat by himself, which wasn't unusual. He drank orange juice. Gene came over and sat in a seat facing Sammy.

What's going to happen.

What do you mean.

I mean, that kid dying on us. What is going to happen.

Nothing.

Nothing.

Yeah, man. Nothing is going to happen. Jim and Jeff will rejigger the rotation. We'll go to the funeral as a team. We'll lose a few more games than we might have won. Nothing.

That's cold, man.

I'm sick, you know, but what can I do. I thought he was going to be one of us. But life's a lie, man. Where I'm from—and this goes for Milwaukee, the D.R., you know—where I'm from, people die all the time, man. Guys like me, Gene. They're murdered. They starve. They die from drugs. They die from pain. They die *in* pain. And nothing ever happens, man. Nothing. Take it from me. Nothing. It's sad, but what is there to do. I know what I do: I say, not me. Not me, man. Not for Sammy. Not for Sammy. No way.

***

Seth, Hector Gonzalez is on the line. Do you want to take it.

Sure.

Hector, it's Seth.

Seth, man. What happened. What happened, man. I just woke up to this crap. Excuse me. I am so confused, man.

It appears he died in his sleep. He may have taken something that was laced with something that killed him. There was no note. No indication, people think, that it was anything but accidental. But he did have a history. He suffered from depression.

You mean he O.D.'d, man.

Yes, Hector. There will be an official autopsy, but that's what we're being told.

Told by who. Did the kid have any family. Oh, this is so bad, Seth. I can't think.

By Mrs. Stefanski. She put out a statement. Turns out she was his legal guardian. That's something I do not think anyone knew.

Seth, man. I think I'm going to be sick. This must be what it was like when Roberto died, man. Oh, I know this is a different thing. But I am sick, my friend. I can't imagine doing tonight's game. There's no way. I just can't. We can't, man.

Hector, we're professionals. That's what we do.

You mean professionals ignore reality. Ignore pain.

I wouldn't put it that way.

Do you think maybe things never change because we're so professional.

***

Jim had worn a uniform most of his days, but this type of combat was new to him. He felt drafted into service. The impending battle jarred vital organs and stimulated dormant synapses. Suddenly, his unit was engaged in a firefight and his foxhole buddy was down. They had been talking— not casually, nothing was ever truly casual during an assault on a stronghold—but they passed information back and forth about the minutiae that inevitably consumes life. And then, with as much warning as any solider gets in a battle, his best mate was down. He's hit. He's unresponsive. Upon inspection, it turns out that he is shot to pieces. Jim's body is in shock, crumpling in on itself. Quantum questions multiply, impossible to locate in any part of his misfiring brain. How many innocents. What deity abrogates to itself. What sense is there on this or any planet. Why hadn't he opportunity to say goodbye. Why hadn't he had the opportunity—the time—to say goodbye.

He awoke face-down on the sofa. He stood and temporarily lost his balance. The oppressive reality about which he had dreamt rushed back and put its heavy boot on him. There was no escaping the pain. He cried so hard that his face began to hurt. Jekyll turned to Hyde and then back to Jekyll. He stumbled and caught glimpse of shock and horror in his gold-rimmed wall mirror, a zombie clinging to life. He recalled fragments of a dream. Sounds of normalcy oppressed him. The globe—its delicately painted gunboat marking the location of Tokyo Bay—mocked him and his life.

He stared deeply at the map and recalled that the U.S. lost over six thousand soldiers on Iwo Jima, the Japanese over seventeen thousand. Twenty thousand more were injured and evacuated, while *fewer than three-hundred Japanese were taken prisoner.* Who won that battle. *What* won that battle. Why was it that we threw away so many young human lives for a speck of dust floating on the sea. Who gave the order, and by what criteria, to spare a few hundred for the sake of war propaganda. It was clear to Jim that part of the calculation must have been a fire sale on human life.

Jim pivoted and drug fingers along spines so thin they felt like petrified wood, *The Little Prince* a bump on a polished log. He thumbed its pages and recalled an unceremoniously grounded author facing death in the vast Sahara. If miraculously rescued, the author might live long enough to share intimate knowledge borne of the gross misfortune he was and had come to know. A message in a bottle. An author who was destined to wash up on shore. Jim stood at the door to the secret passageway, cradling these thoughts. In spite of his rejection of bromides and scouting and the beneficent influence of Mr. S., Jim reckoned that he had still managed to wreck a perfectly good life. This time, it was he who was due up. His fortune cookie read: *like a dog.*

***

Maria Higgins reached over and swung open her passenger's door. Lucy slid quietly into her seat, books pressed to her chest, tears still forming and leaking from the corners of her eyes, a fierce look of defiance camouflaged by an otherwise tender face.

Lucy, dear. I am so sorry.

Mom, it is not fair. It is just not fair.

I know dear. Life, I'm afraid, is often unfair.

Jesus friggin' Christ, mother. No damn bloody clichés, okay. I'm sick of them.

Lucy, please.

Mom, this is serious. That's all I'm saying. Did you read what's online. It's such…. Argh. I can't possibly say. I'm crushed. I'm infield dirt, mom. I'm struck down in a parking lot. I didn't see the car backing out. *I'm sorry, mom, but I didn't see it coming.*

***

As they passed the Badlands, Jeff decided to pack it in. He had an intact family. He was fortunate. He would let Jim know of his decision. Relief scaled Jeff's quivering back.

***

It is with a heavy heart that I confirm news of today's tragedy. Two starts into an all but assured Hall of Fame career, we have lost a player who Mrs. Stefanski herself nicknamed The Little Prince, after her husband's, Aleksander Stefanki's, favorite ballplayer, the late great Hal Newhouser, who was known as Prince Hal. There is not much words can do in such times, although, as with Lincoln at Gettysburg, we might note that what he did here will stand even if what we write does little to add or detract.

***

Dan Higgins stared at his equipment as he waited for his family's return. He flicked at worn apparatus, a World War Two submariner tapping mechanical pressure gauges. Those on-board depended on their proper readings; their indicators foretold that all was well or that a watery grave loomed. Dan monitored them as best he could.

The questions on his mind were submerged in what amounted to the fog of war. Dan had taken a break to consider them, to mark them. Because of what he had lived through, maybe he had a bead on a few answers. Should he share, and, if so, by what art. Dan knew in his marrow that an alive—that is, an alive and awake—human being was greatness personified. It was the prophecy given for each, yet a life-and-death struggle to realize. There were the mounting brute facts of our post -apocalyptic world, like those of our decaying when not outright broken and poisoned bodies. Dan gazed down. Maria and Lucy made their presence known. He called out. I'm in here, he said. I'm still here.

WINTER HAVEN

Winters scoops ground balls and flips to Addison, a miracle of delight and grace. Armando turns from calling ghost runners safe to watch as Durwood cracks a smile. There's Moisés chatting up Prince Hal and The Bambino. Everyone seems to be enjoying the Sunshine State's penetrating warmth and seawater fresh twilight breezes.

Mickey and Hoot, middle easterners, grasp each other's baby's bottom hands. Sammy, whose mood has improved considerably, is pitching never-ending chilled Morir Soñando. Families are here. There are our friends. Waive to family. Waive to friends.

Jim and Jeff, inseparable as ever, meet their Phenom, who is reading a book. He returns sunny greetings and moves directly to join them. Oh my, he leaps over the dugout rail. That he stumbles at the chalk line reassures Jim and Jeff that they are still very much needed. Mrs. S. sees him too. She drapes herself around his firm shoulders.

Akihiko musses the Little Prince's dark hair, making his parents proud. Lester records observations. Someone is looking forward to his first road trip, Hud concludes, comparing notes with his fellow traveler and pointing ahead to their common destiny.

Mr. S. and Rabbi Sloan patrol the outfield. Fr. Heffernan and Mrs. S. join them. They swap stories about Alek's fantastical labyrinth, which they surmise is knowing protestation against mortality. Given their chosen profession, Mary and Sam couldn't agree more. The three human pairs converge near the right field fountains, where they take hold of the most famous of all Japanese watercolors and pursue its watery thesis.

People bustle behind the cage. Members of the press, Hector at the fore, stand ready to tame every willing ballplayer. Others sign autographs for courteous kids, and fans of all ages enjoy babbling baseball banter. Mr. Ross, Reggie, and Willard join Darrell. They put gravy and cheese on their 'dogs and behold Harold's Olympian vigor. Harold lifts home run after home run. Way back, way back, each succumbs. To gravity, and to sparkling resting places undersurface pools of the finest imported champagne.

Three cheers! Three cheers! Three cheers, cries dear Lucy. All hail winter haven.

AUTHOR'S NOTE

"Hey, little prince" were the last words I spoke to my son, Maxwell. He was an eighteen-year-old college student wearing a blue tee shirt depicting *The Little Prince*. It was late afternoon and a gentle rain was falling. Max dashed from his apartment building to my vehicle and I placed five twenty-dollar bills into his hand. He thanked me, mumbled something, and disappeared. Later that evening, he allocated a portion of the de facto allowance to a purveyor of fentanyl-laced opioid. Max was fully and abundantly aware that it was illegal to purchase the drug and that the drug was dangerous, but I do not think he knew, or could have known, that it would be lethal.

Everything and everyone else depicted in this work of fiction bear no such relationship to reality. Resemblances to actual persons, living or dead, or actual events, are purely coincidental.